LUCY
BOOMER

Also by Russell Hill

THE EDGE OF THE EARTH

LUCY BOOMER

RUSSELL HILL

Ballantine Books New York

Copyright © 1992 by Russell Hill

So we beat on, boats against the current,
borne ceaselessly into the past.

NICK CARROWAY
IN *THE GREAT GATSBY*

LUCY
BOOMER

CHAPTER 1

I'm usually out early, try to beat the freeway buildup and get to school by seven, even though I don't teach until eight; so when I go through the pool area in the middle of the apartment complex, there's nobody there, just the empty wire-backed chairs from Yardbirds and maybe a leftover towel or Coke can next to an ashtray filled with cigarette butts. But today there was an owl in the pool.

A great big thing, floating with its head jammed in the skimmer hole, the pool pump sucking at the yellow beak, the wings spread on the surface casting a shadow on the nylon blue of the pool bottom. What the hell an owl is doing here in West Covina God only knows, and how it got into the pool and drowned, if that's what it did, is beyond me.

It floats above its shadow on the chrome blue, pinwheeling a frame at a time, the pool sucking noisily at the beak. The wings are spread as if it's floating in air,

3

but this isn't air, and I put my book bag on one of the chairs and look for the pool skimmer to take the thing out of there. I can leave it for Eddie, the manager, but I can see the scene, some mother goes and pounds on his door and there's a big gathering like when the paramedics arrive at two in the morning and everybody stands in their door and says "What's going on?" to nobody in particular, and then Eddie makes a big production of hauling the owl out, and he'll insist that nobody can swim until he's chlorinated the pool so much that all the kids have eyes that are red and runny and they smell like Clorox. So the simplest thing is to get the bird out of the pool and drop it someplace like the garbage bins behind the student union when I get on campus.

It's heavy, the feathers waterlogged, bending the aluminum pole of the skimmer when I hoist it from the water. It leaves a dripping line on the already warm concrete deck as I carry it by its feet to my car. It becomes a soggy mass of feathers when I drop it in the trunk.

I'm on the freeway in ten minutes. That's one of the reasons I took the apartment, and maybe the only one I can think of that actually made any sort of sense. I periodically think about moving out and finding something closer to work, but I stay here gripped by an ennui that set in sometime last fall when I got the latest batch of Thank You for Your Interest in the Opening in the

History Department of Middle America State College, but . . . and then they tell me in oh so nice language that they've found some Ph.D. in Islamic law who just fits their profile, but not to worry, I'll get out of the sinkhole I'm in if I just hang in there.

A blonde in her forties, skin tight around the cheekbones where she's had her face stretched, driving an electric-blue Datsun Zee pulls alongside, and I turn and mouth the words, "I've got an owl in my trunk. What have you got in your trunk?"

She speeds up, ignoring what no doubt seems like an obscene invitation from a middle-aged nerd in a beat-up Camaro. Sometimes I fantasize that one of these days one of these women I talk to through glass and the freeway roar will smile and pull off the edge and there, with the car nosed into the oleanders, we'll get it on, the rush hour traffic thundering not twenty feet away, just like those letters I read in the *Penthouse* Forum when I browse the magazine rack at 7-Eleven late at night, killing time buying cigarettes and Ho-Ho's, waiting for a woman who's as bored as I am.

It's already hot. Late May, just before the campus lets out, is the worst time, although most of the low cement-block buildings of the community colleges I teach at are air-conditioned.

This morning's campus sits on a flat plain bordered by the Harbor Freeway and a sea of tract houses with small scruffy lawns and silvered Winnebagos in the driveways. Once I saw it from the air and I was surprised to discover how many backyards held pools, although most of them were round dough-boys set on patios.

The owl's feathers are plastered down, and it's surprising how tiny the skull is, the scarred beak jutting from the delicate shape, the eyes grayed and cloudy from the pool chlorine like those of a blind old man. The trunk of my car stinks of wet feathers. I drop it in the yellow debris box behind the student union.

CHAPTER 2

I'm what's called a freeway flyer. That means I teach six hours at one community college, but that's not enough to make me full-time, so I get paid hourly wages, no benefits, and obviously it's not enough to pay the rent. I scrounge three hours at another college out in the valley and teach a night course at a third one in Long Beach. Every semester it's the same, and the asshole exploiters who run the California Community College system keep us running because we're cheaper than full-time professors. Freeway flyers is the polite name. We're the field niggers of the system. When I was a kid I worked one summer picking grapes in the Central Valley, and I keep thinking about how I'm still doing piecework; being paid by the box, hustling every time a semester ends, trying to get enough work to make it through the next one.

I know a guy who teaches in L.A., Long Beach, and San Diego; he teaches sixteen hours, but he must put two thousand miles a month on the beat-up Chevy he drives, just getting to work. We all hope that next semester, next fall, sometime, one of the permanent profs will drop in his tracks and we'll be the one that gets the brass ring.

When I got my master's degree in history (thesis: "America's Decline 1929–1939; The Party's Over") from UCLA, I went right out and got a job at Citrus Community College, started paying off my student loans, married Mary Lea Stanton, who had been going with my best friend for four years and figured life with a college professor was the ultimate step upward. But she had tea in the afternoon at an ivy-covered faculty club in mind, and we ended up in an apartment over a surfer who played his bongos half the night.

At the end of the year I went back to grad school to get my doctorate, and somewhere along the line Mary Lea wandered off with a real professor who looked vaguely like her father. When I finished the Ph.D., I went looking for jobs, but they had suddenly dried up. So now I'm a freeway flyer. I've been one for twelve goddamn years, I'm thirty-eight years old, my hair is thinning, and about five times a month I think about going to truck driving school.

In a way, this morning's dead owl and I have something in common. When I think of owls, I think of forests, quiet, a softness of wilderness that's utterly foreign to where I live. I think of that owl, looking for prey in a field of concrete and asphalt, waiting for the field mouse to run, but there's only cats and sometimes rats that hang out in the crawl spaces under the apartments. This urban owl died, maybe not so much of old age or lack of food, but perhaps because it, too, simply couldn't find its place. Or found itself out of place, searching for woods that no longer exist. I don't want to sound dramatic about this, because at any given moment I could quit trying to teach, and sell cars or insurance, but something keeps me searching for a sense of place in my life. What I do is a long way from being dumped in the debris box behind the student union. But there's got to be more to my life than gridlock on half a dozen freeways five days a week.

Thinking about the owl unnerves me a bit. It's as if somewhere, at some time that I didn't notice, the script for my life got changed; somebody rewrote the rest of it, and all the actors around me have new dialogue, yet I continue to mouth the old words, look for scenery that isn't there, wait for cues that may never come.

I should think hard about the owl, I tell myself, and I should get off my ass and out of this play that I'm in because the end of this one may be all wrong or, worse yet, it may never have an end.

I get my book bag from my car, lock it, and head

for the classroom. Maybe the owl will bring me some sort of perverse luck. This afternoon, between Compton and my class at Long Beach tonight, I'm going to drive to Tarzana and find an old woman named Lucy Boomer.

CHAPTER 3

I ran across the name Lucy Boomer in the Hoover archives while I was researching a paper I hope to get published in the *American Historical Journal*. She was his secretary from 1929 to 1931. And then I found her name mentioned in Schofield's work on Taft, just a casual reference. I remembered meeting Schofield at the Huntington Library once, a short man, odd guy, the kind who leaves your name at the front desk with a note that the book you wanted on the anatomy of penises is out of print. I figured he was approachable, so I called him at Cal State San Bernardino, where he's the head of the history department. He tells me that Lucy Boomer is in a convalescent home in Tarzana, she's in her nineties, she's not all that lucid, and she probably doesn't remember anything about Taft or Hoover, but I figure, what the hell, find her, talk to her, maybe I can get that little edge in this paper that'll get it noticed by the editors.

Any time you get some little chunk of original material, they perk up their ears. Dirt. Any crumb over-looked by the first team, that's what gets the paper into print. For the guys at the universities, it means the road to tenure, or the road up the ladder to full professor, but for people like me, it means having a little red flag on your résumé, something to point to when the sharks swirl around a job opening. There's a feeding frenzy when a good slot opens up, all these Ph.D.'s slashing away, and the guy who's doing the hiring sits back, waiting for the winner to surface. You need something nobody else has, and something like a Roosevelt mistress or pulling some-body's Secretary of State out of the closet is what it takes to convince them you're the one they want.

So we spend hours in libraries painstakingly turning over every rock, hoping we'll turn over one that's been missed by other scholars, watching the sowbugs scurry and hoping that one of these days we'll turn one over and there'll be a genuine scorpion waiting, its tail stiffly curled, or maybe the soft newt of a sex scandal blinking in the light, and we can get it into print in the *AHJ*. And that means that maybe we get to read the paper at the annual meeting. So when we sit across the desk from that old fart who does the hiring, we'll be the one he remembers from the convention, the flash-in-the-pan who found the scan-dal that guys like Schofield missed.

Which is why I'm going across L.A. to find an old woman in a convalescent home who took dictation from two presidents. Maybe.

CHAPTER 4

The elevator opens. In front of me is a nursing station, a white-uniformed nurse seated behind a low counter filling out a form on a clipboard. Two black nurse's aides, round-faced and plump, sit in chairs on opposite sides of the space, like motherly ebony bookends. The floor is filled with wheelchairs, each chair containing an old woman. No, an ancient woman. There are no men anywhere, either as patients or orderlies. In fact, the only man I've seen in the building is the man with the belt full of tools who passed me in the lobby downstairs when I first entered.

There is no order to the positioning of the wheel-chairs. They're scattered in haphazard fashion, some with their backs to the wall, others facing a wall or the duty nurse or each other. From somewhere behind a wall comes voices singing a hymn accompanied by an off-key piano, the player adding gospel riffs in the pauses. The walls of the room are a soft pink, and there's a bulletin board behind the nurses' station with a neatly lettered BIRTHDAY'S THIS MONTH sign and beneath it some balloon cutouts of construction paper in various colors with women's names scripted on them.

The duty nurse raises her head, cupping her chin in one palm, her elbow propped on the desk, waiting for me to cross to her. I ask if I can see Mrs. Boomer, and she says, "Are you a relative?"

"Sort of," I say. I'm not, of course, but the way she asks gives me the impression that if I am a relative, I'll be given carte blanche that might be denied to me if I say no. And, it's simply too complicated to explain why I want to talk to her. She points to a woman in one of the wheelchairs, a tiny bent woman slumped forward, as if asleep, held upright by a cloth harness tied around her waist and knotted to the chrome frame of the chair. All of them, I see, have these same cummerbunds tied around their waists.

The women are all dressed. By that, I mean none of them wear hospital gowns. They're in skirts and blouses and print dresses, but something is wrong, and then I realize that their clothes are hopelessly out of fashion. They have on the kind of clothes my grandmother, who died when I was a teenager, used to wear. Some of the blouses are stained, and one woman's bright flower-print dress looks as if it's on backward. But I don't think any of them know or care that their clothes are soiled or askew.

I'm not prepared for the scene in front of me. It reminds me in a macabre fashion of one of those *National Geographic* specials, or maybe a Marlin Perkins *Wild Kingdom* program. I don't mean to sound flip, but I feel like I've wandered into a museum of old people.

Another old woman reaches down to the wheel of her chair and starts it forward, her legs moving, soft-soled slippers shuffling as if she's walking, or as if the legs work through some memory pattern that moves them only because the body inches forward. She moves aimlessly, perhaps only to move, since she stops facing the blank wall next to a door marked LINEN, and she remains there staring at the wall.

Her face is like the others, almost prehistoric, the skin stretched tight over the beaklike nose. The skin is almost transparent, a bone china shine to it, mottled with age spots. Their mouths are invariably open, eyes set deep within the sockets of skulls that have little flesh on them.

Another chair moves as someone else shifts position. I watch the chairs approach each other slowly, the movement only barely perceptible, a ritual dance as if these creatures, far older than the building in which they live, search for some contact; but when the wheelchairs come front-to-front, they only pause, the old heads swiveling slowly to acknowledge the presence of the other.

I'm struck by the similarity in appearance to the

desert tortoises, their shoulders rounded, their hands on the wheels of the chairs moving the way a tortoise lifts its leg, patiently, deliberately, as if it had all the time in the world, the head thrust forward, the eyes fixed on something or nothing at a distance from them.

When I was a kid we had a tortoise. It lived in a cardboard box in the kitchen, and after the novelty wore off, it was largely ignored, lettuce cuttings from the salad dropped into the box from time to time. It ate the same way these people move, with a slow languor, its little beak chopping half-moons from each leaf.

A woman in a walker spots me and cries out, "Help me, help me," but the duty nurse calls out, "You can help yourself, dear," without even looking up from her clipboard, and the old lady mouths the words a couple of more times silently, as if she's tasting them, and stands there dumbly.

Lucy Boomer doesn't look like a winner. But here I am, and I've sort of said I'm a relative, so I can't just turn around and walk out. Small, she reminds me of a bird in a nest, too young to fly, her mouth open, looking up toward the light now, her sparse hair uncombed, or perhaps the nurses have made an attempt to comb it and there simply isn't enough hair to cover her small head.

There's a plastic chair next to her, and I sit in it in order to look at her at eye level.

"Lucy Boomer?" I ask.

Her mouth closes a bit and she moves her head toward me, her eyes meeting mine. Her mouth moves as if she's forming words, and she makes a whispering noise, but I can't make sense of it. I bend my head down, my ear close to her lips, and again she says something, but it's no use.

I sit back and at that moment her hand clutches at my wrist. The hand is birdlike, the bones delicate as the tiny bones of a sparrow's leg, her skin soft and cool as tissue paper. There is an intensity in her fragile grip, as if she's afraid that, having failed to hear her, I will rise and cross to the elevator and, with the closing of the elevator door, will disappear as quickly as I have appeared in her life.

She looks again at the light, her head back, her mouth open, a thin line of clear spittle drooling from the corner of her lip. I want to wipe it away for her, but I have no handkerchief and I'm not sure she's still aware that I'm there. Perhaps the grip on my wrist is no more than the grip on the arm of her wheelchair might have been. The nurse looks up when I speak.

"Have you a tissue?" I ask. "For her."

The nurse gives me a patronizing smile. "That's all right," she says. "She doesn't notice."

I feel suddenly angry. Whether or not Lucy Boomer notices the drool on her chin is beside the point. *I* notice it, and I'm angry that the bitch can't be bothered to hand me a Kleenex. Surely Lucy Boomer must feel this embarrassing spittle running out of the corner of her mouth like some infant unable to care for itself, and common courtesy would dictate that it ought to be wiped off.

"May I have a tissue, please?" I persist.

The nurse smiles again. She explains the obvious to a child, and she forms her words carefully; too loudly, I think, although maybe years of talking to deaf old people have given her a permanently loud voice.

"There's really no point. She has Bell's palsy and she can't control that side of her face."

"Humor me," I say. The nurse's smile loses its brightness. She rises from the desk, an exaggerated movement designed to accentuate the fact that I've challenged her professional judgment and I'm obviously wrong, but she brings a small box of tissues and sets them in Lucy Boomer's lap. I take one and carefully wipe her chin.

A slight pressure of the hand on my wrist, a tightening of the tiny clawlike fingers tells me that she *has* felt what I have done, *has* heard the exchange, and I am torn between feeling an elation that she has heard, thus proving Nurse Hardass wrong, and an acute embarrassment that she has heard and understood the demeaning way the nurse has treated her. In a sense, I have, by my meddling, brought attention to her infirmity.

She leans forward again to speak, and I bend my

head down to her mouth. The voice is louder this time, no louder than the rubbing of palms together, but I can make out the words.

"Who are you?"

"John Rabbit," I reply. And then, for no reason, I correct myself. "Jack." Using the name I haven't used since I was in high school when everybody called me Jack Rabbit, except my mother, who hated the nickname. "I'm a teacher," I add.

She remains motionless.

"Can you hear me?"

She nods her head slowly. The hand tightens on my wrist. And then, as if she takes some strength from me, she speaks again, this time more clearly.

"Do I know you?"

"No. I'm a teacher. Another teacher named Schofield gave me your name. He told me you were a secretary to President Taft. I was hoping you'd be able to tell me about it."

She doesn't move.

"I know it's a long time ago, but I was hoping you might remember some things. I'm writing a history paper." I'm trying to keep this as simple as possible, and I realize that I'm beginning to sound like the nurse, talking as if I were questioning a child.

She still doesn't move.

Jesus, I'm asking her to remember something that happened maybe seventy years ago.

"Yes," she whispers. "The big one. And then the war came and I worked for that one, too."

"You mean Wilson? Woodrow Wilson?"

She nods.

I feel the adrenaline surge through me. Schofield hadn't mentioned that she'd worked for Wilson.

She nods again.

"Can I talk with you about them, Mrs. Boomer?"

"Lucy." The name comes up like the rest of her words, a slow balloon that rises from her, barely heard above the noise of the air-conditioning vent above us. A nurse's aide squeaks past pushing a cart full of dirty linen. The old woman in the walker mechanically calls out, "Help me, help me," and the aide rubs her arm affectionately, absentmindedly, as she passes.

Lucy doesn't answer my question, so I prod her a bit.

"You can remember President Taft and President Wilson and President Hoover?"

Suddenly it dawns on me that Harding and Coolidge came between Wilson and Hoover. Jesus, is it possible that she was in the White House through five administrations? It's a twenty-year period. It's possible.

"Yes." The word floats up.

"What do you remember?"

"I remember everything," she says, and I'd swear she's smiling, except the left side of her face droops with a sagging paralysis, so I can't be sure.

Next to Lucy an old lady begins to sing "Jingle Bells" in a quavery voice, then trails off. Lucy pushes my wrist in her direction and says, "She's not crazy. None of us are. We just act that way." And then she sags forward against the cloth harness, the effort of three consecutive sentences apparently too much. She stays that way for nearly a minute, the pressure of her hand lessening, and I figure she's drifting off. I watch the red second hand of the clock on the wall opposite the nurse's station and wonder why, in this place of forgotten ancient people, they have a clock with a second hand. I take one more shot.

"What did you do in the White House?"

She raises her head and looks resolutely at me. The eyes are clear—they're not like the owl's eyes— they're sharp and black and intent.

"I fucked five presidents."

At least that's what I think I hear. This ancient woman, semicomatose in a wheelchair, old enough to be my grandmother's mother, says what sounds like "fucked," and more than that, she's attached the verb to five American presidents. I put my ear next to her lips and say, "What did you say, Lucy? Say it again."

And the whispered voice, like rice paper and corn silk, says, slowly, trying to bite off each word as best she can, but unmistakably, "I fucked five presidents."

21

CHAPTER 5

Jesus. Either she's crazy or senile, or inside that shell of a human being is a sense of humor that refuses to die. Or, least likely of all, I've struck the Historian's Mother Lode. I don't even know what to say in response. I'm sitting there, knocked on my ass, and she just looks at me with those black little eyes. Actually, they're not black. They remind me of a brooch my mother had with a bloodstone set in it. Heliotrope, my mother called it, a polished dark brown with black flecks. The drool slides from the corner of her mouth again. She squeezes her hand tight on my wrist so that I can feel my own pulse throb, and her voice is loud enough so I don't have to lean down.

"I kept diaries."

The crooked mouth rises on the right side, and I know that she's grinning, but whether she's playing with me or telling the truth, there's no way to know.

"Where are they?" I venture.

"I was born in Iowa."

"But you have the diaries?"

"I went East when I was a young woman." The voice is fading, slowing, like one of those windup Victrolas, but I can't find the crank to wind her up again.

"Are the diaries here or in Iowa?"

"You'll come and see me again, won't you?" she asks. "You remind me of Robert."

(Who the hell is Robert?) "Will you show me the diaries?"

Her voice has dropped to the papery whisper again. "I can't seem to do it right."

"What, Lucy? Do what right?"

"I can't seem to die right."

Christ, now I'm losing it. Or maybe I never had it. Maybe there aren't any diaries. Lucy's hand relaxes and her head tips back, eyes fixed at the overhead lights, her breath rasping. I wait. No use. She's completely out of it.

I wait a while longer, but she remains in that position, her breath evening into a dry snoring sound, although her eyes are open. The nurse at the desk is looking at us.

"Are you a grandson?" she asks.

"No." Then a quick lie. "She's a great-great aunt on my mother's side."

"I haven't seen you here before."

I shake my head.

"She never has visitors. At least not since I've been here."

I can tell she's fishing around.

"I told my mother I'd look in on her. I'm only in L.A. for a short time."

"How nice of you." When I don't say anything, she adds, "Where are you from?"

"The East." The less I say the better. In fact, I can see it's time to move on. The "help me" lady rescues me. She's got hold of somebody's wheelchair and is attempting to shove it out of her way, but the occupant protests, holding the wheels hard, rocking the chair back into the walker, making angry little whimpers as she struggles. The nurse rises to untangle them, and I take the opportunity to escape.

"Perhaps I'll stop in again," I say, punching the elevator button and studying the polished stainless surface of the door until it opens. Behind me the nurse is busy.

"Be a good girl, Mrs. Lexington, let go."

In the elevator I turn and I see her prying the fingers up one at a time as the door closes.

CHAPTER 6

In my family there were lots of secrets. I didn't know my father had a glass eye until I was thirty-five. By then he was dead, and my mother mentioned it somewhere in a rambling recollection of my childhood. Sounds stupid, but it's true. I just thought he looked at me funny, like one eye didn't work right. That eye looked straight ahead, bored into me when he chewed me out for some transgression, but I never got the feeling that it wasn't live. In fact, it seemed more alive than his good eye that moved independently, darted to one side or the other or fixed itself on me, turning to match its glass brother. Wall-eyed, my great aunt would have said.

It wasn't a conscious secret, something that was kept from me. My older brother knew. It's just that the family was close-mouthed.

"What they don't know can't hurt you," my mother used to say, which is why, I think, I'm such a good liar. Poor liars run off at the mouth. They get caught up in a web of contradictions. In my family there were a lot of silences. Dinners were funereal affairs, punctuated by the sounds of forks against plates. I remember going to the Antonellis' house for dinner when I was a teenager and being shocked by the noise. They shouted at each other, argued, accused each other of old indiscretions in an attempt to gain the upper hand. I thought they were the angriest people I'd ever seen or heard until I realized that the Antonellis hid nothing from each other.

Most of us aren't like the Antonellis, I've discovered. There are gaps in our lives, missing pieces that somebody else is able to fill, but the piece is squirreled away in a hidden pocket in the back of the brain, like a critical piece in a puzzle that lies on the card table, mostly put together, but there's a piece of the face shaped like Italy that you can't find, and in the back of your mind you wonder if maybe it's lost, on the floor, or they just forgot to put it in the box at the factory, so you go on and on, turning over pieces looking for Italy rather than going ahead with the rest of the puzzle. All the while the piece is in someone's pocket or purse, saved for a time when they can use it. Or maybe never use it. Just the idea that the piece is there is enough.

CHAPTER 7

The class: there are just enough students to cover the enrollment limit. Any less than fifteen and they cancel it, and a couple of times in my illustrious career I've had friends enroll when it looked like I was going to lose one of these night classes. That was back when there was no enrollment fee, but now the state charges fifty bucks just to drop in, so that's no longer an option for me. They never bothered to come to class—I just carried them on the roll until the third or fourth week, then dropped them as soon as I knew the class was locked into the schedule. It's not that I don't care about the teaching itself—I do care. I like teaching, and I like making people come alive over some scene out of the past. I like it when they listen to me tell them about the Ghost Dancers at Wounded Knee and see them sit up and know that inside their heads they're suddenly saying to themselves, "Jesus, this wasn't in my high school history book," and I actually get chills sometimes when I describe a scene like the one where Custer asks his Indian scout what the outcome of the day will be, and Bloody Knife says, "Death," and the class is so quiet that I know I've done more than just recite some facts.

Night classes usually fill with housewives and students who work full-time during the day, and the usual inevitable assortment of college junkies who show up year after year. On the positive side, they all want to be here, or most of them do, and some of them are history buffs as well, so they're pretty well-read. On the negative side, they're usually so miserably tired by the time a seven P.M. course rolls around that by nine o'clock they're drifting off into never-never land.

We're supposed to go until ten, but I give them a long break after an hour and I usually start winding it down by nine-thirty. Any earlier and the conscientious ones may bitch about it on the end-of-semester evaluation forms I'm required to hand out.

Night classes like tonight, when I've taught in the morning, and I know I've got an hour on the freeway after class, are the toughest. There are times when I go on auto-pilot and I can hear myself talking or reading a passage aloud and at the same time I'm thinking about something entirely unconnected to the subject. It's like my voice is disembodied, floating out there with a life of its own while inside I take little side trips to keep myself awake. I'm actually afraid that some night I'll go to sleep standing behind the lectern, just trail off like one of those hypnotized idiots in a Las Vegas lounge show.

In this class there's a couple of mousy kids that look like the kind you find behind the window at Jack-in-the-Box; male or female, it's hard to tell them apart. A big guy in sneakers the size of snow shoes who's in his twenties—nice kid who keeps telling me about the Lakers and the Raiders during break. I can't tell if he's really interested in talking to me or just trying to drag the break out longer, but he doesn't know that I don't care how long we drink coffee out of paper cups in front of the vending machine.

And Mrs. Watson.

Lonnie. "Please call me Lonnie," she says. All right, Lonnie. No problem. Lonnie is about forty-five and she owns a boutique "out in the valley" and she's divorced and she just *loves* history and she thinks I have a *wonderful* voice for lecturing, all of which she managed to say in one sentence during the break the first night of class, except the part about her age. Lonnie tends to wear spandex tank tops, and the sight of those big jugs of hers in the front row in metallic-blue or pink or maroon is disconcerting, to say the least, but I've assiduously tried to avoid her at break.

Guys who teach night classes call them sharks. Bob Wilcox, who teaches a class in beginning computers down the hall the same night, and who usually has a beer with me afterward, keeps telling me to ship her down the hall for some mathematical enlightenment.

"Christ, Rabbit, she'd go down in the parking lot before you could get the car door closed," he says. "What the hell's wrong with you?"

"She's not my type," I say.

Actually, it's not that at all. It's just that these people are distanced from me and I have no desire to close that distance. There's a protection in seeing them as numbers that show up in class and then disappear. I don't want to know why the sneaker kid can't be bothered to do the reading, and I don't want to know why the Jack-in-the-Box kids never ask a question, and I don't want to screw Lonnie Watson.

Bob Wilcox has high blood pressure. He looks laid back, and he talks slowly, kind of a drawl, and you'd think he was the most easygoing person in the world, but it's because he's full of all these drugs. He's a walking pharmacy, filled right up to the eyeballs with diuretics, tranquilizers, all kinds of downers, because if he doesn't take all this shit, he's going to explode; just blow up, his arteries balloon up and go pow! and his heart comes right out of his chest like a fist. Like in that movie *Alien*, where the creature comes right out of the guy's chest and the audience goes nuts. Wilcox keeps talking about getting laid, but I wonder if he can get it up with all that stuff in him.

Lonnie's a shark, and then there are the "spinners." Wilcox explained that to me one night. We're having a beer and the waitress comes up, a wiry woman in her thirties, and she leans over to wipe off the table. She's got on a cotton T-shirt and her little tits show when she reaches across. Wilcox turns to me and says, "Spinner," and after she leaves I ask him what the hell he said.

Spinners, he explains, are insects that come up through the water to shed the shells of their pupae, using the surface tension of the water to shuck the outer garment of skin, rising into the air with a spinning motion as they emerge as adults.

To be a spinner, according to Wilcox, a woman has to be small and slender—in fact, she borders on the skinny, and she has a certain frenzy about her, the kind of woman who'd shriek and laugh at the same moment she comes. Maria, the department chair's wife, is a spinner. I remember her at a department party one Christmas. She came wearing a green silkish blouse, the blouse loose at the neck, a gold chain knotted at her throat, and she literally gyrated when she danced, like those crazy dervishes who play polo with the sewn-up heads of vanquished enemies after a battle, the kind of dancing that's frenetic, as if the sexual energy is about to explode.

I have this sudden image of Lonnie Watson sucking Wilcox off while he's eating pills by the handful, like M&M's, until finally he runs out of pills and boom!

he explodes like some Roman candle, and that's it. Except it leaves her thinking she's some kind of spider woman, and from then on she's really careful since she doesn't want to kill anyone else. Or maybe she goes around looking for more bodies to chalk up on her leotard, and wonders why she can't blow anybody else away.

I look at Wilcox and I think maybe I should take drugs, too, only what I need are uppers, something to put the fist in my chest. But I cannot seem to get up the energy to do even that.

Mostly I'm stuck on center in my life. Which is why I can't seem to get up whatever it takes to move from my apartment. The classrooms I teach in are grubby, so much like the classrooms where I spent time in high school, except that there are ground-out cigarettes on the floors, and the venetian blinds are usually askew, the cords broken, and at night everything is bathed in a harsh neon light, and I don't even think of myself as a college teacher anymore, just an itinerant peddler who punches in to lecture and punches out again, like some sort of academic factory worker. My lack of movement right now stems from this feeling I have that no matter what I do, things won't really change.

Every once in a while I see a woman who lives in Claremont. Her husband is a hot-shot investment banker and he travels a lot. They've got a house in the hills, and I went up there the first time with a woman who teaches at Compton who got invited to dinner. One thing led to another.

So every once in a while I see the banker's wife. Mostly we sit in her hot tub and watch the coyotes run through the tract avenues below her house. The tub hangs on the edge of the deck, and at night the coyotes come out of the San Gabriels and go loping down the avenues, strange dark doggy shapes that run loose-jointed under the streetlights. When they built the homes up to the edge of the mountains, the coyotes, being nobody's idiots, didn't leave. They found that stray cats and dogs and garbage cans were a hell of a lot easier pickings. They come down in little packs of two or three, sliding through the avenues and the backyards, past the station wagons and bicycles lying on their sides in the driveways. And the banker's wife and I sit on the edge of the deck, steam rising from our bodies, and watch for them. We make love in the hot tub. I've never seen her bedroom. I simply pass through the house. I suspect I'm not the only one, but it suits me. We have no real connection. We rarely talk.

CHAPTER 8

Wilcox asks me again tonight if I'm going to bang Lonnie Watson. I think he's asking permission to do it himself, although what makes him so damned sure the woman is hot to trot is beyond me. I leave after one beer.

I don't mind driving the Harbor Freeway after ten. It's usually cleared up that late, a few red taillights, every once in a while the bright glow from the big green overhead signs, like little oases. I like to open the windows and let the air whip around inside the car, turn up a Spanish station full crank and rip along like an imitation low rider. I like the idea that I don't have to pay any attention to the Spanish words because I don't understand most of them. The Spanish DJ raps along, and if I squint my ears, the rhythm is the same as in English, every once in a while an English word like "K mart" or "Ford" jumping out. You'd think that after thirty-eight years in L.A. I'd have picked up some Spanish, and I do know about a hundred words, but most of them you'll find on restaurant menus.

I think about Lucy Boomer. About the diaries, if they really exist. Suppose they do. Suppose the old lady really did what she said she did. I do some mental arithmetic. Schofield said she was in her nineties. Let's say early nineties—maybe ninety-three. That means if she went East like she said, she might have been eighteen or twenty. A term for Teddy Roosevelt and another for Taft puts her in her mid-twenties when Wilson comes around. Mid-thirties for Harding, late thirties for Coolidge, and early forties when Hoover shows up. Christ, it's possible she worked for six presidents!

I try to imagine what she might have looked like when she was younger, but there's nothing to go on. Except the eyes. The lid on the paralyzed side of her face droops, giving her a lopsided look like a cloth doll that's been stepped on, but the polished brown irises like my mother's bloodstone brooch—there's something about the eyes that's compelling. Maybe she has pictures of herself.

Lately I've been reading Conrad. He talks about the empty white spaces on the maps. Unexplored places. In the same sense I see the empty spaces in people's lives. I suppose it comes from digging around in history, trying to fill in the gaps, but I've never been terribly interested in events. I'm fascinated by photographs. Not just my own scrapbook that has childhood pictures of me and Ray and Art and my dad standing by the waterfall at McCloud while my mother snapped the lever on the box Brownie, but photographs of everyone. Photos in boxes in antique stores; old photographic postcards in junk shops; shoe boxes of glass negatives wrapped in tissue; stern-faced sepia-toned photos of farm husbands and wives in chipped gilt frames sold at flea markets for the frame, and each time I look at the faces, the man standing next to his new team of horses proudly showing them for the camera; another man leaning on his bicycle, his trouser legs tied with cord; two women on the running board of a touring car holding their hats to their heads, their white dresses billowing around them, and the name of the photographer scripted diagonally across the bottom, *Marion Studio, Rock Island, Illinois, 1923*. And I wonder where they went that day, make up little narratives: the photographer is the brother of one of them, the other is her friend. Or is she his friend? I imagine Lucy as one of those women. It's easy because there is no resemblance. The old woman in the rest home is, in a sense, like the ashes of a fire, still warm, but gray and dying. No way to reconstruct the fire from that.

CHAPTER 9

Crossing the apartment house patio, the pool lights are off. The water is black, a child's white flotation ring with a duck's head drifting in the center, suspended in the darkness. There is the smell of chlorine and cooling concrete mixed with the leftover smoke of somebody's barbecued hot dogs drifting down from one of the balconies.

A man and a woman are arguing somewhere above me, and their voices get louder as I go up the stairs, and I know it's the couple who live just above me. It'll go on until about one, and then I'll hear just his voice and the slamming of doors and drawers and the hall door, and a few moments later she'll peel out of the parking lot, lay a lot of rubber, her last statement. It happens about once a week. I've never seen them. She calls him "asshole," and he calls her "bitch." Those are about the only understandable words I ever pick up. She always comes back. The argument muffles when I close the door except for the stomping feet on the ceiling. I turn up the TV to drown it out. The TV runs all the time. Sometimes I watch whatever's on and I rarely change the channel except to watch the ball games.

My apartment's a pigsty. That's what my mother would say. I used to be really neat when I was married to Mary Lea, but last year that began to slide. I gave up on sheets for the bed. A sleeping bag lies on the exposed mattress on the floor of the bedroom. I've got cardboard boxes along the wall of the living room, where I keep my clothes. In the middle of the mess of papers and books scattered about the floor is the table where I work. There's a little galley kitchen adjoining but I don't use it much except to cook stuff like canned corned beef hash. Little round doggy burgers with an egg on the top. Mostly I eat out.

I find an empty glass and rinse it out, fill it with ice cubes and gin. Beer gives me a headache. It didn't used to, but somewhere in the last year I began to get blinding headaches after I drank half a dozen beers, and when I cut back, they disappeared. I'm okay with gin.

The news is still on, and some jerkoff with a funny hat is pointing out big whorls on a weather map behind him. Tomorrow's going to be sunny, he says, and whips out this big yellow smiling face and covers up Southern California. Big deal, tomorrow's sunny for the next five goddamn months. For this he probably makes eighty grand a year.

Last night I read in a bulletin from Johns Hopkins about some neurologists who were working on theories of memory. They had this guy who got zapped when he was trying to change the electric heating element in his kitchen stove. When he wakes up, it's August 1945, and he thinks he's fourteen years old. This fifty-year-old guy suffers an electrical thunderstorm in his head and thirty-six years of his life go up in a puff of smoke. And it wasn't just *things* he remembered. He began to *act* fourteen. He thought his kids were older than he was, talked like a fourteen-year-old, didn't like green beans. His wife filed for divorce.

I can see the bolt hit and go skimming through his brain, little blue puffs of smoke vaporizing his kids, his wife, his new Toyota, his bowling scores, Kennedy, Ike, high school, leaving the smell of burned electrical insulation hanging inside his skull like an electrical drill that's been overheated.

What the Hopkins people discovered is that memory is chronological. It's all lined up in a row from the time you're born. If memory were organized differently, say, according to subjects or smells or tastes, then that electrical bolt would have left disconnected pieces of memory intact. But this guy's jolt told them it's all lined up like dominoes, standing on end in a long line stretching back for years.

Upstairs the doors start slamming. Early departure tonight.

Memory is a narrative, like a novel. It's not a bunch of filing cabinets in the brain arranged under smell or place or alphabetically. Kick one of these neural dominoes and they all start to fall.

If I can get Lucy Boomer to retrace the river of her memory, maybe I'll have something. But it means I've got to get her to go back through forty years of other shit just to get to Hoover. Unless, of course, she lied about fucking five presidents. It'd be enough if she did it with one.

She called me Robert. Does that mean she's already stepped back in time, started working her way back through her memories, so that it's not really the spring of 1981 for her?

CHAPTER 10

The smell of urine is pervasive as soon as the elevator door opens. It's not as bad as a service station bathroom, but it's there without any doubt, an invisible ammonia sharpness that's in every breath. The rest home is neat, almost spotless; in fact it resembles a hospital, at least on the floor where Lucy lives. I have no idea what's on the first two floors. I come in through a small lobby where a woman sits in a glass booth with a telephone and a sign-in book, but she's always buried in a magazine and I doubt if she'd recognize me, even if I came every day.

The urine smell comes from the fact that some of the old women wet their beds. And some actually wear diapers. I only know this because I overheard two of the black nurse's aides in the elevator bitching about doing old white ladies' diapers.

Lucy remembers me from last time. First she says, "Hello, Robert," and then she adds "Jack," as if I have two names. She's more alert today. Although her voice is hard to hear, the words come more quickly. They don't have that slow-floating balloon quality they had the first time I was here. It's earlier in the afternoon. Maybe that makes a difference.

They're trying to get Mrs. Lexington to take an afternoon nap. She resists, just like a child.

"I'm not tired. I won't go."

"Don't be difficult, dear."

She holds tight to the railing that runs along the wall.

"No! You can't make me."

Pry at the fingers. Plead.

"Come on, sweetheart, you'll feel better after a little nappie."

"No!" Petulant.

The nurse is getting pissed off. Lucy asks me to wheel her to her room. Perhaps the scene bothers her.

Her room is split by a curtain hung on an overhead track. On the far side of the curtain someone groans. Lucy's bed is high, hospital style, steel crib rails along the sides. A bedside stand has a lamp but no personal effects. No pictures, no comb, nothing. The only other object is a white cord with a call button the size of a shotgun shell. The bed is tightly made, tucked in almost brutally along the edges, military style.

The window is on the far side of the drawn curtain, leaving Lucy's half of the room darkened. There is no place for me to sit, unless I let down the bed rail and sit on the bed.

"Do you mind if I sit on the bed?"

She waits in the wheelchair.

I let the crib rail down and it suddenly plummets with a metallic bang. Lucy doesn't move.

"Can we talk about when you were in the White House?"

"You remind me of Robert."

"Who's Robert?"

"Sometimes it's hard to remember." When she speaks, she continues to look straight ahead toward the nightstand, and I reach out and gently turn the wheelchair so she faces me, but because I sit on the the high bed, she faces my knees. She raises her head and looks at me.

"Was he your son?"

"No."

"Do you have children?"

"No."

"What about Mr. Boomer?"

"My father was a dancer."

"You weren't married?"

"No. Never."

The room is warm, and the gray wool blanket under my outspread palms feels scratchy and sweaty. Lucy's hands pick gently at the edge of the cloth cummerbund that fits snugly around her middle, idly pulling at it much the same way you'd twiddle your fingers, her thumb and forefingers pinching it and stroking downward. She's wearing a thin blouse of shiny material, one button unbuttoned halfway down, a stain just above it that looks permanent. The blouse looks as if it might be silk that's been carelessly cleaned, or perhaps laundered by mistake.

Despite the heat, she says that she's cold, would I get her a sweater? Where is it? I ask.

She nods toward a closet next to the door, but when I try it, I find it's locked.

"Is there a key?"

"In my pocket."

Her skirt has no pockets, but there's a cotton bag hanging from the back of the wheelchair. Inside I find some crumpled tissues, a pair of reading glasses, a dollar bill, and a key on a string.

The closet is nearly empty. Two or three blouses and a couple of skirts hang on wire hangers, a pair of scuffed black women's pumps with low heels are on the floor, and on a shelf above the blouses is a worn sweater, a shoe box with the lid taped down, and a small leather suitcase, the corners scuffed and raw. The initials LAB are embossed on the case under the handle.

I drape the sweater over Lucy's shoulders, and for the next hour she wanders through her memory, not responding to my questions, as if this is a tale that she will tell in her own way, one that cannot be abridged;

how she came to this place in 1970 when she knew she could no longer care for herself, first to the little apartment with a sitting room on the first floor, later to the third floor from which no one leaves alive, she tells me.

"The diaries, Lucy," I ask during a long silence, thinking about the shoe box with the taped lid. "Do you still have them?"

"Yes," she says. "You'll come again to see me, won't you?"

"You'll show them to me?"

"I have to go to the bathroom. Call someone."

I push the call button on the table, and a few moments later one of the aides looks in.

"She has to go to the bathroom," I say, and the aide wheels Lucy out the door. I wait on the bed, the silence broken only by the ragged snoring from the other side of the curtain. I think about looking in the shoe box. I wait.

The aide wheels Lucy back into the room.

"She's going to take a nap," the aide says pleasantly, untying the cotton restraint around Lucy's waist. She takes her under the arms and hoists her into a standing position. Lucy grabs the rail at the end of the bed to steady herself, and the aide begins to unbutton her blouse, as if she were undressing a child and not a woman, assuming, I suppose, that I'm a close relative and that it won't matter if I see the old woman naked.

I'm startled at what she's doing, and for a moment

I can't seem to move. She peels back the blouse and Lucy's tiny breasts, no more than sagging nipples against her delicate chest, appear. I want to look away but I watch for a moment and I'm struck by the fact that her skin is smooth, like alabaster, not at all like the patchy parchment of her hands and face.

"I should go," I say, looking deliberately away and sliding off the bed.

"It's good when they have visitors," the aide says, talking to me as if Lucy weren't there, as if she were undressing a doll or a mannequin. "Ain't many relatives willing to spend more than a few minutes with them. I hope my boys are as good to me." Obviously she's noted the fact that I've been here for more than an hour.

"I'll come and see you again, Lucy," I say.

"That'll be nice," the aide answers.

CHAPTER 11

This afternoon, driving to the rest home, I cut across through Venice. The palm trees look silly, skinny sticks that tower above the sidewalks, little brushes of tops like feather dusters. They're about as natural as eye stalks on one of those aliens in a Saturday morning cartoon. And the light smashes off the fronts of the stuccoed bungalows, brilliant, darts off windshields of parked cars, hurts my eyeballs even though I'm wearing shades. I think about stopping in a bar someplace where I can find darkness.

At a stoplight on the corner of Ranchero and Sunset, I see the monkey. He's in the window of an ugly apartment house that's on the opposite corner, one of those square stucco things with flush aluminum windows, the drapes stained, or maybe sheets hung across them. And there's this monkey, a little one, his face pressed to the glass. At first it looks like a stuffed animal, but he clutches the drape with his little fist and

his head follows a woman on the street below, watching
her pull her child along, the kid dragging, the mother
sweating, holding a bag of groceries crooked in one arm,
jerking at the kid's arm, and above her the monkey
watches, shifting to look out the corner of the window
until she's out of his sight.

There's something pathetic and very wrong about
the monkey in the window. Venice is full of weirdness,
girls on roller skates in bikinis that aren't anything more
than a string between their cheeks, and old guys with
anchovy breath and skin that looks like alligator lug-
gage.

They sit in the sun on benches, hunched over like
Lucy in her wheelchair.

It's funny, but I never noticed them before. Now
I find I look for them. Their skin is almost black from
the sun, but they wear long-sleeved shirts and old sweaters even on days like today. Their faces are like the
monkey's face, pinched and wizened, and, like the monkey, they seem to do nothing but wait and watch.

Somebody honks behind me. The light changed.

CHAPTER 12

I've taken to visiting Lucy twice a week now. July in
L.A. is one day after another of dry heat, hazy smog
that turns the San Gabriels into blue smoky lumps fading in the air. I sit around the pool at the apartment
watching the mothers and kids, the kids in baggy diapers leaving wet footprints on the concrete that evaporate almost as soon as they appear, the mothers, most
of them in their early thirties, trying to hide the lum-
piness in their thighs.

My checks stop when school stops, and I've got a
summer job three days a week in a Fotomat in Placentia, a little booth in the middle of a flat black asphalt
lot, blue with a yellow roof, just big enough for me and
about ten thousand rolls of film. It's air-conditioned,
but I usually turn the thing off and leave the window
open, sit there and read, wait for cars to come up, leave
off film to be developed, pick up pictures. They always
open the pictures before they drive off, shuffle through

them, sometimes shove one out at me as if I gave a shit, anxious to share with a total stranger some moment at the beach. I've had guys show me a picture of their girlfriend, stark naked on the table in the backyard, sitting there with legs crossed, tits hanging out, and say things like, "Not bad, huh?" and I'm not sure they mean the quality of the picture or her boobs, although it seems hard to imagine that they'd shove a picture of her boobs at a total stranger and say something like that.

Maybe it's something about the car/booth relationship. Like I'm not really a person, and they aren't either. This is the second summer I've had this job, and once I got started, I got interested in the number of places in L.A. where you can do things without leaving your car. The obvious ones are places like McDonald's and Jack-in-the-Box, but you can get tacos and Greek food and buy milk and eggs, drop off your laundry, pay your electric bill, do your banking, get drugs, both legal and illegal, mail a letter, make a phone call, and there's still drive-ins alive out in the valley where you can see a movie, and, I suppose, screw in the backseat. I read somewhere that in Atlanta some undertaker has a drive-in window so you can see the deceased without having to get out of your car. The weight of the car activates a curtain that slides back, and the coffin is tipped at an angle so old Uncle George is visible, and you don't even have to put on your pants or take out your curlers to pay your last respects. I can't figure out why that's in Atlanta and not in L.A.

Anyway, I go visit Lucy, spend an hour sitting on the edge of her bed, listening to her, the shades drawn in her room, the woman on the other side of the half-drawn curtain that divides the room snoring, occasionally moaning, soft little moans that at first alarmed me, but now I've gotten used to them. They sound like the noises dogs make in their sleep.

There is little furniture in this room. The hospital beds with their chrome rails are too high for these fragile old women to climb into without help, and when they lie there napping, a cotton strap ties them down, lest they fall onto the vinyl tiled floor. Beside each bed is the same metal stand and plastic pitcher. Only the lamp on the stand in each room is different. Beside Lucy's bed is an old piano lamp, the brass plating rubbed away in places, the fluted shade blackened where a bulb has burned it. It is the only personal object I can see. Some of the women have hung pictures on the wall opposite the end of the beds, framed photographs of grandchildren, mostly. And a few rooms have chests with the occasional television set on top. That much I can see through the always open doors as I come down the hallway. But in Lucy's room there are only the lamps. It could easily be a hospital ward, except for the rose-colored walls.

Lucy calls me Robert, and she speaks in the present tense, even when she's describing something that happened long ago, as if she's there, watching it. She knows I'm Jack. I remind her, and she says, "Yes, I know," but when I come in each time she says, "Hello, Robert," and I've stopped correcting her.

I've returned to the subject of the diaries a couple of times, but she stonewalls me on that one. They exist, she tells me, and I'll get to see them, and then she drifts off into reveries that touch only occasionally on the White House, but mostly about her childhood on the farm.

This afternoon she goes on about the sky, how dark it gets when storms approach the farmhouse, the lowering of the clouds until the prairie seems sealed to the sky, the receding grain darker now, the wind making waves in it, the heaviness of the air, until I can see the grain move, feel the oppressive humidity, wait for the crack of lightning. She can see her father framed in the doorway to the porch, looking out across the field toward the approaching storm. If it's a bad one, it'll beat the grain to the ground, ruin the crop, but he waits patiently. And when she stands beside him, he says, "Nothing's a sure thing, Lucy. It's all very delicate and it can get beaten down in a minute. You remember that. Nothing's permanent. Not me or your mother or Robert or even this house."

His overalls smell of cows and dust. "Can you smell it, Robert?" she asks me.

CHAPTER 13

Some of them are wheeled out on the sidewalk that leads to the rest home on these hot July afternoons. Despite the blinding sun they're usually covered with a blanket and, hunched over, they're like terrapins sunning themselves. Like the ones that sit on old boxes or bits of trash washed down during the storms into the wide concrete ditch of the Los Angeles River, where pools of sluggish water have gathered behind pockets of silt.

The old people terrapins, their mottled skin the color of the mottled shells of the turtles, hunch in their wheelchairs on the sidewalk. They wear dark glasses, all of them, dime-store models, bright red and yellow plastic frames stuck on the wizened faces so I can't see their eyes, only the black glass patches parked on their noses like Groucho Marx disguises.

There is a ringing in the air on days like today, a hard brightness that the smog can't diffuse. The colors fade, the trees and bushes take on an olive shade, lines are drawn with a hard, sharp pencil. The bright red and yellow sunglass frames look as if they've been pasted on this hot Southern California postcard.

Times like this I half expect that when I walk through the door of the rest home I'll find it's only a facade—a Hollywood back-lot false front, and on the other side will be timbers propping up the whole absurd scene. But inside the building it's cool, the lobby always has two or three of the more ambulatory old women sitting in chairs, wearing gloves, purses at the ready, poised as if they're about to go someplace. Sometimes they actually do, when a relative arrives, usually a middle-aged woman who looks vaguely like the old one.

It is semidark in Lucy's room, and she lies on top of the tightly made bed, hands at her sides as if she were laid there, not moving. She's not asleep. When I bend over the bed to say hello, she says, "Hello, Robert. Jack." Each time I get two names.

I sit in the wheelchair at the side of the bed, wheeling it close enough so I can hear her. Because of the height of the bed my face is level with her head. When she speaks, she talks to the ceiling, not bothering to turn to me.

She is in Iowa today. The last time I came she talked about Hoover, how he liked a bowl of fruit in the room wherever he was, even when he was on trips. She went with him once, she said, to Rio de Janeiro. It was Carnival and she dressed "like a butterfly," she said, with a bright yellow mask that she held to her face with a stick. Her voice grew animated when she spoke of the midnight festival, the dancing and drinking until the sun came up, everyone in costume so that there was no way of telling who you were dancing with unless they spoke.

Today she's in Iowa. She's sixteen and she walks through the crackling cornfield, the serrated edges of the leaves brushing at her face, toward the thin line of trees that marks the creek. It isn't much of a creek, just a trickle that runs under a cut bank of clay until it meanders out into the pasture. She takes off her clothes and lies in a shallow pool, the slow water barely covering her naked body, and she looks up through the thin green trees. The cows, curious, gather at the creek to watch her.

As she speaks to the ceiling I can almost see the faces of the cows gather around her bed. The faint urine smell in the room becomes the smell of the animals, a cow smell that fills the air. Her body, lying on the bed, becomes the slight naked body of a teenage girl lying on her back in a shallow pastured pool. The water moves slowly over her shoulders, parting her hair.

And then, she says, she ran down the avenues of the corn in the July heat, the water drying from her skin almost immediately, terrified lest her mother find her running naked through the field, running until she was slick with sweat, finding herself back at the creek where her clothes were, finding her brother Robert sitting by her clothes, naked.

I loved my brother more than anyone or anything, she says. Her hands move for the first time, stroking her thin thighs. We never spoke, she says. He went away after that.

A sliver of sunlight comes past the corner of the curtain, and as the sun sets, the pale yellow sliver begins to disappear, the shadow of the sill slowly nibbling at it. I use it to mark time, listening, hoping she will say something important, but today I'm lost in her story and realize with a start that the sliver is nearly gone, only a tiny bright slice left near the ceiling.

Lucy turns her head on its side to look at me. "I want you to take me from here."

Jesus! My first reaction is that she wants to live with me.

"Lucy," I say, "there's no way I can take care of you. I live in a studio apartment that's three flights up. I'm gone most of the time."

"No," she says, her head turned so that the lopsided part of her face is buried in the pillow, the animated half talking to me.

"I don't want you to take me to your home. I want you to take me to Iowa."

"Why?"

"Get the box from the closet."

"The shoe box?"

"That's right."

I put the box on the bed between her face and the edge and open it. Inside are a pair of old-fashioned woman's hair combs, curved with long teeth, the tops carved to look like ibis or storks entwined. They look as if they're made of ivory. There's a necklace of round jade beads the size of marbles, a bundle of canceled checks, a folder with the name of an insurance company in scrolled letters, a contract with the name of the rest home in block letters, and a small packet of photographs. No letters, no diaries.

"The pictures," she says, and I untie the string around the little packet of photos.

"Find the one with the children."

I shuffle through the packet. Several postcards, a photo of a young woman in a beach chair, the ocean over her shoulder, wearing a white sundress, looking boldly at the camera; another of a group of young men in their twenties, dressed in work clothes, standing in front of the drive wheels of an immense steam locomotive; and a photo of three children spaced evenly apart facing the camera, a painted canvas backdrop behind them with the outline of a Mississippi River steamboat crudely drawn. At least that's what I think it is.

The three children are in blackface, the smallest in the center wearing a top hat, the other two taller, one wearing a derby, one a workman's cap. The smallest looks about seven or eight, the others a few years older. All three are dressed in men's clothes, but the jackets and shirts and pants are not baggy—they've been altered to fit these smaller bodies. There's a watch chain draped across the tallest kid's chest, and the kid on the opposite end leans slightly to one side, away from the others, wearing a long workman's coat of some kind. The bigger ones hold axes, the smaller one a hand saw. They appear to be three boys dressed up for some sort of theatrical event, but the little one wears high-button shoes that have a distinctly feminine look about them, and the face, despite the sooty black covering that leaves only white eyes and the gray slit of a mouth, is delicate.

I look at the old woman lying on the bed, look again at the photo of the young woman at the beach. They are the same, yet not the same. I do not see Lucy in this picture, I recognize her. It's as if a police artist had worked backward, shaping a face and body that would have been Lucy, if only the witness had been closer, had been able to see in the light of the white beach the features that lay in the half darkness on the hospital bed next to me. And, extending those lines, the way Mrs. Steers used to take lines to a vanishing point in art class when I was in junior high, almost at the vanishing point is this small child in blackface, a hint of Lucy's cheekbones in her delicate face, the eyes like two white almonds with black pupils. She stands closer to the taller boy, who is stiffly at attention.

"I'm the one in the middle," she says, confirming my guess.

"Robert is next to you?"

"The taller one."

"Is it a play of some kind?"

"A minstrel show. My father taught dancing."

"I thought he farmed."

"Yes. But he was a dancer before he came to Iowa. When he was a young man." Her voice has an urgency to it, a strength that surprises me. She speaks to the ceiling still, but there's no need to strain to hear.

"He built a big shed on the corner of the farm next to the county road," she goes on. "He called it the Prairie Moon Ballroom. People came from miles around to dance." Her crooked face smiles. "He taught them how to waltz. His real name wasn't Boomer. It was Sheck."

At first it sounds like "Sheck," but I realize that she has said Czech, as in Czechoslovakian.

"I want to die there, Jack." This time she's got my name right. Her head turns on the pillow to look at me.

"Lucy, I can't just take you to Iowa. It's two thousand miles away."

"You can have the diaries." The smile again, as if she's played the trump card, as if now I have no choice.

"Lucy, I can't take you."

"Yes you can. You just take me for a walk in that damned wheelchair and go around the corner and get in your automobile and drive me to Iowa. You do have an automobile, don't you?"

"Yes."

"Then it's settled." She turns her head to look at the ceiling and seems to sink into the pillow, closing her eyes.

"Lucy, dammit, I am not going to take you to Iowa."

No answer.

Reach out and touch her arm. The first time I've touched it, and it seems so frail, the skin soft, no hardness of muscle, nothing but the membrane of skin and tiny bones.

But she still doesn't respond. I suppose it's ten minutes before I leave, go out past the sunglassed terrapins, leaving her snoring in the dark room, the acid smell of urine still clinging in my nostrils.

CHAPTER 14

Back when yards had little cement trolls in them instead of plastic flamingos, and Monrovia was mostly
orchards, we used to come back from some relative's
house on Sunday afternoons, all the windows open, the
hot air flowing in and around us, my brother and I in
the backseat, my parents in front. My father always
drove, and my mother used to reach along the seat to
stroke the back of his neck, massage the base of his
neck as he drove, both hands gripped on the wheel. I
don't ever remember them showing much more affec-
tion than that. I can close my eyes and imagine her
hand, the slim gold band on one finger, kneading at my
father's neck, his head black against the white of the
windshield as we drove toward the sun.

And it was in Monrovia somewhere that we always
saw the dog. It was chained to a fence in a vacant lot.
When we came to the stop sign opposite, the dog would
lunge until it came to the end of the chain where its

body snapped around, sometimes throwing itself on the ground, only to rise again and lunge against the end of the chain, barking fiercely at our car.

My father always said something like, "Goddamn owner ought to be chained up there for a while, see how he likes it."

The lot was empty except for the brown grass and weeds; a wide semicircle next to the fence was worn to the dirt outlining the dog's radius. When the dog lunged, the dust would fly up, lighting in the slanting sun, the dog lunging again and again in the dun cloud. When the car started off, the dog stood, watching, and I always watched out the back window to see if the dog lunged at the next car, but it seemed as if he never did.

I imagined the dog lunged only at us. That he waited, sometimes for weeks until we would arrive, as if by magic at his corner, where he would rage at us until we were gone again.

And then one Sunday the dog wasn't there.

"I hope the poor sonofabitch got loose," my father said, and we all knew he meant the dog that wasn't there. We never saw the dog again. After that, my father used to make up little stories every time we passed the vacant lot. How the dog had stowed away on a Dollar Lines ship and had gone to Hawaii where he grew fat on pineapple and lay in the shade all day. Or how he had hitched a ride with some Mexicans and was now, at this very instant, lying on the beach at Vera

Cruz lapping fruit punch and tequila from a flowered bowl.

My father worked as a bookkeeper for a lumber company. He went off every day to a job I never understood. He "kept books," whatever that meant. And then, when he was fifty-three, he had a heart attack and he was gone. Like the Monrovian dog. One day he wasn't there.

I was a teenager when that happened. I never really thought much about what happened to him. He died. He didn't go off to Hawaii, where he never went when he was alive, or to Mexico, although once we all went to Tijuana for a day and came back with serapes and huge straw hats and a case of the trots that tied us all to the toilet for a week. Now that I think about it, the stories about the dog were really stories about him. He, too, wanted to stow away in a Dollar Lines ship. When we were really small he used to take us to the docks in Long Beach on Sundays to look at ships, and he built little models of them for a while. I can see him on the beach at Vera Cruz, rubbing the neck of that Monrovian dog, his pale shiny shins reddening in the tropical sun.

And what had my father raged at? Nothing, as far as I know, except his outbursts at the absent owner who chained the dog to the fence. But my mother, only a couple of years ago, corrected me when I referred to my father as "mild-mannered."

"No," she said. Once, for a whole year, he carried a huge tractor nut on the ring with his office keys, expecting to be fired by the bastard he worked for, and he was going to throw the keys with the metal nut on them through the boss's office window. He had it all planned, but then he had the heart attack. She showed me the nut, clean and shiny; it must have weighed half a pound.

This afternoon in my little blue-roofed cubicle I squint at the parking lot. Heat shimmers the supermarket across the street. The chain that ties me to this place is of my own making.

CHAPTER 15

I tell Lucy that I've decided to take her to Iowa, and we agree that Saturday will be the day. It's when relatives descend on the home, take people out for shuffles, bundle the lucky ones into station wagons. We'll get a day's head start. Lucy maintains, that I'm not kidnapping her; she's all for it, but we both know that as soon as they discover she's gone, they'll start looking for her. And for me. Checking herself out of the home is simply too complicated a task. There's no way they're going to release her to me. I'm not a relative and I'm not about to take on financial responsibility for her. I can't. Besides, I figure we'll be back in a week and a half. I think about trying to arrange a "visit" to someplace for her, without Lucy knowing about it. Just tell the people who run the home that she's going to visit some relatives. That way we don't burn our bridges behind us, but it's silly to even think about it. Nobody's going to buy that kind of lie from me. I'm not even who I pretend to be when I visit her. When I ask her if she has relatives in Iowa, she says yes, but that's as much as I get out of her.

Still, I figure we'll drive to Iowa, she'll see it, we'll drive back. Four days each way. A day there. I'll slip her back into the home and I'll have the diaries and that's it. What was it Goethe said? Something about "learn to seize good fortune."

I raid my bank account of $800, most of what I've saved for the September money drought, have the car serviced, and let Eddie, the apartment manager, know I'm going on vacation and won't be back for a couple of weeks.

But there's more to it than just the diaries. I've grown attached to her. Sometimes I dream about her; sweaty dreams where her old-woman face shines like a porcelain doll. And when, in those dreams, I strip away the clothing, the body is not the frail old woman body I see lying on the bed in her room, but a childlike body, the head and neck attached like an old-fashioned doll. I am drawn to the body, want to caress it, slip my hands over it, but it is a child's body, and even though the woman face urges me to take her, I cannot.

I wake, hard, throbbing, and I go and stand in the shower in the dark until I come, the water flooding over me, knowing that the faint echo of the water rushing through the pipes half wakes my neighbors, who, perhaps, feel the thumping of my heart and mistake it for the thumping heart of a husband or wife.

And then, drained of energy, I lie in bed and think about how the only passion in my life is generated by a ninety-three-year-old woman who is, perhaps, lying awake at this moment—and the accidental web that drew me to her.

Saturday. Everything seems sharper today. I'm conscious of the receptionist in the glass booth on the first floor of the rest home. It seems as if every aide says hello, as if they're memorizing my face, looking at their watches so they'll remember the time.

"Yes, I remember exactly when they left. He wheeled her out the door at exactly 11:42. I remember because I looked at my watch right after I looked directly into his face."

The duty nurse smiles when I wheel Lucy to the elevator, and turns back to her clipboard. Under the shawl that covers Lucy's shoulders and lap is the shoe box, the only thing she wants to take. Nothing else, she insists.

Outside, the sidewalks already smell of hot concrete, the sky taking on that hazy L.A. tinge that I know is brown only because I've seen it from the air, but from the ground is a nondescript filter that softens the sun without lessening its heat. The car is around the corner, and when I open the door, the sudden release of hot air is oppressive. I lift Lucy from the wheelchair. She's light, really childlike, and I put her in the front seat, wrapping the seat belt around her. She clutches the shoe box the whole time.

The wheelchair won't fold up. It won't go in the backseat. Finally, in desperation, I put it in the trunk. The lid won't close, so I tie it down with the cotton sash they used to tie Lucy to the wheelchair.

Lucy is sitting up as straight as she can, looking just over the dashboard, and it reminds me how tiny and vulnerable she is.

"Okay," I say. "Iowa, here we come."

She grips my wrist.

Pigeons, gathered on the curb pecking at birdseed thrown there by one of the old people, swirl up, wheeling in the sun, disappearing in the white center, reappearing as they settle on the wires above us, then drifting down in twos and threes to strut about in the grain.

And then we're off.

That's what my father used to say when we set off on our Sunday drives.

The wheelchair in the trunk is a problem. It's a giant sign announcing Lucy's presence, and even though they'll have no idea of what kind of a car we're in, the half-open trunk with the wheelchair is a red flag I've got to ditch. It occurs to me that I could dump it in the dropbox where I dropped the dead owl last spring, but if anybody finds it, they may connect it with Lucy's disappearance, and they'll suspect foul play, as they say in the detective novels, and then things will really hit the fan.

I'm already feeling paranoid about this whole situation. Lucy doesn't help. She says nothing when I speak to her except, "Drive faster, Robert," or "Drive faster, Jack," so I stop trying to make conversation and concentrate on getting us through the freeway traffic, aiming north toward 395, past Palmdale and on up over the summit to Bishop. Where the hell all these people are going on a Saturday morning is a mystery to me.

The farther we go, the more I think about the damn wheelchair, until it seems like it's some huge wart on the back of the car that everybody sees, comments on, and then they memorize my license plate.

Finally, at an empty rest stop the other side of Newhall, I pull over, take out the wheelchair and carefully back over it several times until it's flattened, the wheels crumpled and the shape almost unrecognizable. Then I toss the whole thing over the edge into the poison-oak-filled gully below. Anybody who sees it won't bother to go after it, that much is sure.

Back on the road I feel better, and we drift up 14, coming closer to the edge of the Mojave. Past the Palmdale reservoir, on the outskirts of Lancaster, I ask Lucy if she's hungry, but she says no. I stop anyway at a Quik-Stop and get some sodas, and we sip them in the hot car, the windows open.

We stop for gas in Rosamond. The dry lake glitters off to the right, flat sandy desert stretching between here and Soledad Mountain, the gray round mass that means Mojave isn't far off.

Lucy says she still isn't hungry. She has to go to the bathroom, and I carry her into the men's room in the service station, set her down on the toilet seat and hold her so she won't fall in.

Jesus, she's so thin that the big seat which has this cutout on the front is hardly small enough to keep her from falling through. I sort of stand her up in front of the seat, and she tries to get her pants down, but she can't seem to, and there's this embarrassing moment when she realizes she can't do it, and I realize I'm going to have to do it for her, so I get down on my knees and she leans against my back while I pull her pants down around her ankles. They're damp, and I realize that she's wet herself sometime during the morning, but the heat of the desert air has helped to dry her out. Christ! I want to just cry.

When I stand up, she slides her hands down and lifts her skirt, settling back jerkily onto the toilet, and she nearly falls through, except that I catch her around the waist and hold her. She looks straight ahead, and I look at the back wall of the stall. There's the sound of her peeing, and then her body begins to shake, little soblike jerks, and I know she must be crying.

But her breath comes in little gasps, and she's laughing. Little squeaky burping jerks of laughter, and then her voice, weak, but each word carefully enunciated.

"It's been forty years since a man did that."

"What." My voice squeaks, too.

"Pulled down my panties."

She starts squeaking again, holding on around my waist, me holding her, and then I'm laughing, too. It occurs to me somewhere in the middle of this that if anybody comes into the men's john and finds me and this old lady clutching each other and laughing while she's sitting on the toilet, that we're going to do more than raise some eyebrows.

I pull her up and help her back into her underwear. Her eyes are red, the lopsided grin spreads across her face, and when I pick her up to carry her back out to the car, she holds on around my neck, more like a girl than an old woman.

But the laughter dies quickly. The afternoon wears on, Lucy dozes, wrapped in a blanket in the backseat to protect her from the hot air that blows in. I've got the windows open, it's blistering hot along the edge of the Indian Wells Valley. Off to the right the Argus Mountains rise out of the sandy plain, dun-gray in the shadows, brilliantly lavender where the sun strikes.

There's an interval of green as we approach the little town of Brown, and the irony of that isn't lost on me. Then across the Owens River, dropping into a valley where, I suddenly remember, I went on a field trip years ago when I was in grad school. Way up on the bluff are the carvings of hundreds of tracks on an unscalable wall, carvings of infants' feet, bears, dogs, coyotes. The Paiute obliterated a lot of them just before the turn of the century, claiming they'd been made by evil little men who'd crept from the rocks at night. I remember climbing up there with the class, sweating, using binoculars to pick out the remaining carvings. I never did figure out what it had to do with the class, except the instructor was one of those hippie leftovers from the sixties who wanted us to get a "hands-on" feeling for history.

It's getting dark when I come out of the Inyo forest on the far side, with another seventy miles to the Nevada line. I've got a headache from not eating; Lucy still sleeps. When I try to talk to her, I get no response, and once I stopped the car to see if she was okay. I figure I'll stop in Tonopah, where we'll eat, find a place to stay, and sort all this out.

CHAPTER 16

Tonopah. The dust is flying. The wind comes across the desert and the dust flies. A newspaper flaps across the parking lot like Quasimodo, all hunched over, and then gets pasted to the window of the diner. The light from the streetlights and the floodlight on the single pole in the parking lot is yellow, thick, and the air is warm and dry, like a giant hair dryer that keeps blowing, rattling the street signs and making the wires hum. When we came into town tonight there was lightning playing off the land, sheets of it and sometimes crackling lines that touched down, and the almost smell of rain, the ozone that fills the air, making me lightheaded, and the car radio crackling like mad, hissing and spitting every time the car filled with the eerie light when the horizon lit up.

I turn off the engine and sit for a minute. Next to me a huge livestock truck rumbles, diesel idling, the driver gone somewhere, the pigs in the back stinking and oinking and rattling against each other, squealing, maybe sensing they're going off to some pig Dachau. Lucy's asleep in the backseat now. Maybe she's dead. Christ, I don't know. I don't know how the hell I got myself into this. A ninety-three-year-old woman who's comatose half the time, and if it weren't for the pigs, I could smell the urine where she's wet herself again. I need help, that's all I know. And a cup of coffee.

Inside, the wind stops humming and it's cool from the air conditioner, that kind of clammy cold that comes with plastic air. The café is full, counter crowded, the booths along the window filled. I look for a place to sit. There is only one person in the booth at the far end. A young woman sits there, staring out the window, a cup of coffee in front of her. My car is opposite her, and she must have seen me get out of it. I look out through the window, but Lucy can't be seen. She's still asleep. The girl turns to look at me, then turns back toward the window.

Her hair is extraordinarily long. Even though she's sitting down, I can tell that it's long. It falls over her shoulders and some of the strands fall loosely over her forehead and face and spill onto the table around her elbows. The electricity in the air has charged her hair, and some of it flies out to the sides. One hand holds it out of her eyes and at the same time, pressed to her forehead, holds her head up. On the back of her hand is a five-pointed star, tattooed just above the knuckles, the size of a quarter. It looks as if it's been hand done.

There's something odd about her, something that doesn't quite fit. She wears a loose blouse over her thin torso and a wide, hippie sort of skirt around her in the booth. Her face is thin, almost hawklike, with an intensity that's apparent even though she's just sitting there staring out the window. It's like the electricity that charges her hair comes from inside her, as if all I have to do is touch her like when you go across a carpet and you touch a doorknob and it gives you a shock. The counter is full of men, truck drivers, maybe some locals, hunched over coffee, trading lies, so I stand at the edge of the booth and say, "Excuse me."

She looks at me disinterestedly.

"You mind if I sit here?" I lean my head at the counter. "Everything seems to be taken."

"Go ahead," she says. She looks out the window. I can see the car where Lucy sleeps. Everything's yellowish outside, dust flying, like it's some sort of huge weird television set with the color all screwed up.

I order coffee and a hamburger. The girl stares out the window. The window shakes when the wind hits it. A newspaper slaps against the window, then skids off and disappears. I can see my car from this window seat. She holds both hands around her cup. The waitress brings coffee for me, fills the girl's cup again.

"You heading east?" She's speaking to me, although she still looks out the window.

"Yes."

She looks at me. "How far you going?"

She is not pretty, but there's something about her face and her body, as much as I can see of it, that's striking in a disturbing sort of way. She's in her twenties, maybe late twenties, now that I can see her face more clearly. No makeup, and she keeps pushing the mass of dark hair back from her forehead with one hand, twisting her fingers in it, letting it loose to fall again over her slightly inclined face, only to push it back again.

It occurs to me that she's angling for a ride. Obviously I look harmless. Or manageable.

"I'm not traveling by myself."

"Damn. Just my luck. Look," she leans forward. "I need a ride. I keep to myself. You wouldn't even know I was there."

"You could probably get a ride with one of them." I nod toward the men at the counter.

"Yeah." Her voice is resigned. "But I'm not interested in screwing my way to Chicago."

"I've got my grandmother with me. She's in the car asleep."

She perks up. It occurs to me that she's exactly what I need at this point. There's a balloon over my head with a light bulb in it. She needs a ride, I need help with Lucy. It's not as if she's been waiting here all this time for me to park in front of that window and come in and ask to sit at her table. It's another goddamn accident, and I need to seize it before it fades.

"I'm not going all the way to Chicago."

"How far?" She leans forward, her hair draping across her coffee.

"Iowa. My grandmother's very old and she's going to stay with some relatives."

She's looking to one side of me, and I realize that she has this nervous habit of looking to one side or the other, her hands always moving, kneading her hair, hovering around her coffee cup like moths, her long fingers spread, then closing.

"Look. If you want to, you can ride with us. But my grandmother is very old and I need some help with her."

"What do you mean, help?"

"Help in getting dressed, going to the toilet, stuff like that."

Now she's cautious again.

"I'll tell you what." Plunge in. "I'll take you to Chicago if you'll help me with her as far as Iowa."

Her eyes are darting around now, not sure she likes the smell of this.

"She's out there in the car?"

"Absolutely. If you don't believe me, you can go out there and see for yourself. Look . . ." It's my turn to lean forward. I'm trying to hold her eyes in one place. I want to grab the sides of her head and make her look right at me. "I need help with her. You need a ride. I'll pay the expenses. All you have to do is give me a hand with her. No strings."

"What's your name?"

"John. Yours?"

"Ahna. With an *h* in it." Her eyes stop darting long enough to get a good fix on me. "Listen," she says, "no weird stuff, okay?"

"What do you mean, no weird stuff?"

"You know, like no weirdness." She darts her head at the men at the counter. "I'll help you with your grandmother, that's it."

"Perfect." The waitress puts the hamburger in front of me. "You want half of this?" I ask. Things are falling into place.

CHAPTER 17

The motel is U-shaped, a gravel courtyard, wide over-hanging eaves covering the walkways. The sign says MO-TEL, but it ought to read AUTO COURT. It has that 1940s look about it, peeling white paint in the dim light of bulbs strung from a single pole in the center of the courtyard.

The room has two double beds and a folding bed, bunched up in the corner like a mattress sandwich. It smells of mildew and Clorox. I put Lucy on one of the beds and turn on the lamp on the table next to it. Old *National Geographics* are stacked neatly on the cigarette-scarred surface. Opposite, a window faces onto the courtyard, and the gravel crunches as a pickup truck moves past the half-open curtains. Ahna flops on the other bed. She carries only a huge red cloth purse with the word Guatemala embroidered on it.

The folding bed springs open when I release the catch, nearly chopping off my foot when the metal feet slam to the floor. When I sit on it, I sink deep, hammocklike, but when I look across at Ahna, she shakes her head.

"No, no, no, no," she murmurs, spread-eagled, arms touching the edges of the bed. "Don't even think about it."

The bedside lamp illuminates her face, and I can see that she bears a faint resemblance to Lucy, what Lucy might have been at that age. Her eye on this side of her face is in shadow, hollow and dark, and it's like Lucy's eyes, set deep back in her skull, so I cannot tell if she is looking at me or not.

Lucy lies still on her bed, her hands at her sides, looking straight at the ceiling. I get up and cross to her.

"Are you okay?"

She smiles her crooked smile.

"Where are we?"

"Tonopah. Nevada."

She smiles some more.

"I like her."

"You mean Ahna?"

"Yes."

I had no idea she was awake when we got in the car at the restaurant, and assumed she slept until I lifted her from the car at the motel.

"She's going to help us."

"I can count on you, Jack." No Robert this time.

"Are you hungry?"

"Yes."

"What would you like to eat?"

"It doesn't matter. Not soup. Something to chew." She watches me for a moment out of the corners of her eyes. "Go on, leave us. I'll be all right." When I hesitate, she speaks again. "Get something to eat that I've seen on television."

"Like what?"

"One of those hamburgers or something like that."

Her voice is so soft that Ahna cannot hear what she's saying.

"I'm going out to get something to eat for Lucy."

Ahna sits up. "Bring me a beer, will you?"

I somehow didn't expect this. If she had said, "Bring me a guava juice or bring me a tofu burger," it would seem more in character. It's the hair and the skirt and the blouse cloaking this woman that fool, and I can only nod.

I walk along the road, stepping on the sidewalk where there is one, walking along the edge of the pavement when there isn't, listening to the buzz of neon signs for motels, car lots. A dog barks, a steady coughing bark someplace on a back street, like an old man's cough, timed almost to my steps, a hacking accompaniment.

Far down the street I can see the glow from the town's casino, but this isn't much of a town, mostly gas stations and funky motels, the occasional sixteen-wheeler grinding its way through town, working its way up through the gears. Ahead is a McDonald's, and when I get there it's still open, although nobody's there except the pair of bored kids inside.

Back at the motel, Ahna is waiting. Lucy is under the covers, the sheet drawn up to her neck.

"Where the hell are her clothes?" Ahna asks.

"You mean they aren't in the car?" I lie.

"What the hell is going on here? There's no bags in the car, she keeps telling me not to worry, she's pissed all over herself, and I had to wash her stuff out in the sink." Lucy's things are spread over the back of the chair in front of the electric wall heater that hums loudly. The room is hot.

"Look, I must have forgot to put them in. We'll buy some new stuff tomorrow. It's no big deal. Here." I hold out the six-pack of beer and the white McDonald's bag.

She stands there, arms folded across her chest.

"I'm not getting involved in any weird stuff, do you understand? She says she's not your grandmother. Who is she?"

"She's my great-great aunt. It's just easier to tell people she's my grandmother. It's no big deal, right Lucy?"

Lucy nods her head and says something.

"What's that?" I bend over her.

"I want to eat."

I start to lift her upright, but she's not wearing anything and the sheet starts to slip down her body. Ahna comes over to wrap the sheet tightly around Lucy, muttering obscenities about weirdness, and once Lucy is erect, leaning against the wall with pillows propped behind her, the McDonald's bag in her lap, I sit on the edge of the bed. I unwrap one of the burgers, and Lucy takes it in her chicken-foot hand, takes a tiny bite, like the bites the turtle used to take. I realize that she seems stronger, not like the woman who sagged in the wheelchair at the rest home.

"Well," Ahna says expectantly.

"Well, what?"

"You. This ancient lady. No clothes. What the hell is going on?"

"Just like I told you. I'm taking her to Iowa where she's got relatives. So I forgot to pack the bags." I hand her one of the beers. "I'm really tired. We can go over this in the morning."

Saying it makes it so. I'm aware, as soon as I've spoken the words, that I am held together by threads, and that if Ahna should clap her hands, I would simply fall apart, spread across the cigarette-burned linoleum floor like so many fish released from a net, the parts of me slithering and flopping, disconnected from each other.

I want to lie on the hammocky folding bed and sleep.

"Tomorrow I'll buy some clothes for her." Lucy has finished the burger and is rustling in the sack for another one, her lopsided face grinning as she chews. At least she's happy. Ahna cracks the beer and takes a long sip.

"I should walk out of here now," she mutters, but she says it resignedly and flops on the bed opposite Lucy.

Everything seems unreal: the cone of light from the bedside lamp that makes its sparse circle on the dark ceiling; Lucy, like some wizened ascetic, her sparse hair frizzing in all directions, the white sheet wrapped about her, rummaging in the McDonald's bag; Ahna, lying back in the bed, sipping at the beer, tipping the can slowly to her lips to let it dribble into her mouth; outside, the drum now of soft rain on the overhang, the steady dripping off the eaves, the rise and fall of tires making their soft wet noise on the street at the end of the court. A man and a woman's voices in the overhung passageway are muffled. I feel as if I can touch this scene—fingers from my brain reach out and fondle the hot dampness of the room, feel the rain slip through my brain's fingers, touch Ahna's thick hair and Lucy's electric hair.

And then we sleep. At least I know I do. If I dream, I don't remember.

CHAPTER 18

Tonopah on a Monday morning: bright, filled with the promise of heat, a hard blue sky. Slot machines clank and buzz and jackpot bells ping through the open door of the Stockman's Hotel. There are mostly empty parking spaces along the curb, and a sense of abandonment or maybe a sense of never was to the shops just opening.

Inside the Lucky Lady Boutique a single clerk adjusts sweaters on a shelf. The store is empty except for the two of us. It smells of cloth. I ask for help.

"Excuse me, I need a skirt and a couple of blouses for my grandmother. Something washable. About size five."

She looks at me expectantly, as if I'm supposed to say something, but I don't know what.

Then she asks in a countrywesterntwangy voice, "Is this for dress-up or just casual?"

"Casual. Just something for everyday wear."

She pulls apart the skirts on a circular chrome rack

and stands to one side. What I want is for her to decide for me, pick something so I can get out of there.

"Something in a cotton? Maybe a print?" She fingers a skirt.

"That looks fine."

"Maybe a denim?" She pulls a skirt halfway out.

"No, the first one looks good. I'll take it."

It's as if it's too easy for her. But Lucy and Ahna are waiting at the motel and I want to get this over with. She shows me a rack of blouses, and I pick off two flowered ones. She takes them from my out-stretched hand, not looking at the blouses, watching me warily.

"Will that be all?"

I'm about to say yes when I see the other blouse. It's a soft, shiny material—looks like it might be silk, and I imagine what Ahna might look like in it. A gift to placate her. She's still sullen this morning, unsatisfied with my vague explanation of Lucy's relatives.

"How about this?" I hold it up and the ivory sleeves shimmer.

"I'm afraid that's not a five," she says. And then, holding up the two blouses and the skirt like evidence, she adds, "And it's quite a bit more pricey than these. It's silk, you know."

"Put it in a separate bag." The extra eighty-five bucks is a little shock I keep to myself, dropping the twenties on the counter as if they're ones. I'd put the silk blouse back if she hadn't made that last remark. Too late now.

Back at the motel Ahna dresses Lucy while I wait in the car. For some reason I don't give the blouse to Ahna. Maybe she'll think it's weird, or that I'm trying something strange. The balance is too delicate to upset, and she seems genuinely concerned about Lucy and just plain pissed off at me, convinced, I'm sure, that I'm lying about everything. Once we're on the road everything's going to settle down. I can feel it.

But it doesn't stay bright for long. The sky turns gray and I have to turn the heater on. Ahna is less nervous than last night. At least her hands move less, but she stays pressed against the door on her side of the car, her head inclined slightly so she can watch the landscape rushing by. She seems to have no interest in the road ahead, which lies straight, bordered by dusty olive-drab sagebrush, broken only by the occasional billboards for a gas station in Ely, almost two hundred miles farther on.

I adjust the mirror so I can look at her face. Even in the daylight she has dark hollows around her eyes, as if somehow she hasn't taken very good care of herself. She's in her late twenties—maybe even thirty—it's hard to tell. She wears no makeup and her face looks older in the morning light. She smells of a heavy musk perfume, almost a sweet animal smell. Her eyes suddenly look straight in the mirror at mine, gray-green eyes that bore into the reflection without blinking, and I look ahead at the road involuntarily, as if I've been caught spying on her.

Attempts at conversation bog down. She just grunts at questions. Lucy sleeps.

CHAPTER 19

At lunch Lucy tells us a story. I don't think she knows where we are, but she knows we're traveling, and that seems to give her a perverse kind of strength. It's not a physical strength. If anything, she's weaker than she was, and I have to carry her every time she leaves the car.

We're in a rest stop in Salt Lake City, it's nearly two in the afternoon, and it's a relief to get out of the car after the long haul from Ely. It's a park, sloping down to some tables where several families have spread picnics. We park at the top of the parking lot and I carry Lucy to the foot of a tree, prop her against it. We spread out our lunch. McDonald's again. Lucy asked for it. Ahna calls it poison, and has some sort of granola bar that she got in a Quik-Stop while I was getting the burgers, but she's got a couple of beers to go with it, which seems strange. We sit against the tree, Lucy wrapped in the blanket—she's always cold, but I am too, and we sit next to each other as much for warmth as for companionship, me on one side of the old woman, Ahna on the other.

Lucy is remembering the horse they used on the farm for haying. Why the hell she's remembered this, I have no idea, maybe it's the grass or the trees. Anyway, she's talking about this horse that used to pull the long rope that went through a block and lifted the hay into the loft. At least that's what it seems he did. She rode on the horse's back, gave the horse commands, told him when to back, when to go ahead. But her commands were unnecessary, she says. "He did his slow dance for more years than I had lived," she says. "He tolerated me on his back like my father tolerated Olaf, the hired man, not because he could do anything, but because he was someone to talk to."

There's something compelling about her voice. I have to lean close to her to hear, and Ahna leans from the other side, caught like I am.

"When I was older," she says, "I used to climb to the loft and work with the men," and the chaff-flung air floats in front of us while she talks. Whispers. I can see the great hall of the barn, the glitter of the dust in the sunlight, the sound of pigeons in the rafters.

"I had a horse once." Ahna breaks into a long silence. There's a lot of silence when Lucy talks. "I took riding lessons." And then she stops, as if she's said too much.

"Teddy rode," Lucy says. "He was the best horse-man of them all. He rode them like he was part of the horse. Once he rode his horse right up onto the porch of the house in New York. It made a grand noise, the hoofs on the porch, all those eastern ladies and their dandies scattered like so many birds to the wind—but there wasn't any danger. He knew what he was doing."

Ahna looks at me. "Who's Teddy?" she asks.

"A brother." No point in telling her too much about the White House.

CHAPTER 20

I'm glad for the overcast skies when we hit the salt flats. The road seems to stretch in a wavering line like an R. Crumb comic strip, endless white with broken fences along the side, salt-saturated posts, pools of stagnant brine and sick-looking shrubs on the edge of the pavement. I half expect Mr. Natural to pop up any moment, spread his prayer rug and warp off into hyperspace.

And I'm glad when the flats end and vegetation, however weak it looks, begins to return. We climb steadily out of Wendover, aiming for Wyoming, and as we gain altitude, the scrubby alkali brush gives way to sage and then to the occasional stumpy tree.

Now weatherbeaten farmhouses appear every once in a while and the land takes a dark turn, the sun no more than a grayness behind us.

Somewhere just west of Evanston two dogs run in a field as we drive past. They're both dark dogs, some kind of farm dog, largish, and they run across the field, circling excitedly, stopping, ranging out again, one of them dropping to a trot, then a walk. The sky is gray. The fields are wet. Stubble from the crop, whatever it was, lies in little blackened windrows on the unplowed field.

I know it is cold outside the car without rolling down the window. It has that cold look. Empty and bleak like a drainage ditch with a cat floating in it. The car is warm, the hot air blowing up from the vent near my feet. I'm sleepy, not tired of driving, but simply sleepy, as if I could put my arms on the steering wheel and go to sleep while the car moves steadily on through September. It is as if winter has arrived here on this plateau, or perhaps winter is always here.

The dogs are the only things moving in the empty fields, except for some birds that whirl up and spiral down again in a black vortex behind a sheet-iron farm shed off in the middle of the field. The dogs are smaller. One of them has stopped, his nose to the ground.

The car drifts to the side of the road, and I let it slide off onto the damp shoulder. The sudden bumping as we go off the pavement wakes Ahna. I turn the car down toward the fence so I can see the dogs.

"What are we stopping here for?"

"I'm falling asleep."

"Want me to drive?"

"No." I roll the window down.

She sits back against the seat, pulling her hair back with both hands, stretching the skin of her face until her eyes are slits.

"What are they doing?"

"Who?"

"Those dogs."

"Looking for rabbits or rats or mice."

"Whose dogs are they?"

"Probably some farmer." The dogs work at something in one of the windrows, noses down, scratching at the dead vegetation. They're close together and at this distance look as if they are only one dog, so that when one of them looks up for an instant, there's a sudden, startling impression that the dog has two heads, one head pushing at the stuff, the other head sniffing at the air.

"I don't see any house."

"Maybe they're magic dogs. They just appear in the field, looking for an abandoned child to raise."

She turns to me, releases her hair, licks her lips. They're cracked and there's a little fleck of scab at the corner of her mouth. The pink tip of her tongue touches the scab, probes it briefly.

"What's that supposed to mean?"

"Nothing. I just made it up."

There's a long pause and the wind rocks the car slightly, imperceptibly, like a tiny earth tremor.

There's a hard edge to her voice when she speaks again.

"Magic dogs. Don't get me started on that shit!"

"Look, I didn't mean anything by it."

"Yeah, but if I had on a pleated skirt and a little middy blouse you wouldn't say things like that. And this." She grabs her mane of hair and pulls it back until the skin on her cheekbones stretches white. "Some kind of hippie earth mother, right? Like I've got some kind of weird powers, or I'm in touch with the center of the universe, or some shit like that, right?"

I'm stunned by the intensity of her voice.

"No, look, I'm sorry. I didn't mean anything by it." The dogs come toward us, galloping, as if attracted by the sound of her voice. One of them has something in its mouth, and as the dog becomes more distinct, I can see that the thing is alive, wiggling, a rodent of some kind.

"Jesus Christ," Ahna says. "It's got something." She slumps down in the seat until her head is level with the dashboard. "Let's get out of here. I don't need this."

The dogs are at the side of the car now, panting, their breath coming in little white bursts. They're a mixture of lab and something with a slightly longer coat, excitedly milling next to the door on Ahna's side, so that I can only see the little clouds of steam, then prancing out into the field a bit. One of them holds a rabbit in its mouth, the legs still jerking. Whenever the rabbit kicks, the dog shakes its head vigorously.

The dog breaths rise in little puffs like comic-strip balloons, but there are no words in the balloons, only the dogs' dumbness, like large mute nephews, the kind you feel sorry for; they cause a vague uneasiness, as if they could be dangerous if they were provoked.

I start the car and wait while a truck passes. The truck seems close, but it takes a long time for it to grow larger and then rock past us, the dirt from the wind swirling around the car. I back onto the pavement and head east again. Ahna slumps in the seat. In the rear-view mirror the dogs grow smaller, watching us, one of them walking out onto the road. I am reminded suddenly of the dog in Monrovia, the one my father made up stories about. I want to tell Ahna about the Monrovian dog, but she stares at the glove compartment, and I'm not sure she'd understand why I've recalled a nameless dog from my childhood. I look over my shoulder at Lucy. She's awake, bundled in her blanket in the corner of the backseat, staring straight ahead at the back of Ahna's seat.

"How you doing?" I ask, twisting the rearview mirror so I can see her eyes without turning my head. She looks at the mirror and nods her head, then closes her eyes. Ahna has curled up against the door, her feet drawn up onto the seat. Her hair blankets her head and back, her face hidden in a pocket formed by her arms and the door.

It begins to rain. Mist at first, then a few drops, finally a steady rain blurring the windshield between swipes of the wiper blades. The slap-click of the wipers is hypnotic, the landscape much the same quality, the fields gone again, long stretches of sagebrush broken by clumps of scrub pine as we gain altitude.

Within the hour the rain begins to thicken against the blades, and an occasional snowflake whips erratically up the windshield, and then it snows, not heavily, the snow melting as soon as it hits the road, the pavement black and dull and cold.

The clouds lift just before dark, the last light breaking through behind us. There are signs along the road now, GAS AHEAD 23 MILES; 65 ROOMS, MOTEL 6; a huge cowboy with a lariat standing in the sagebrush with a sign encircled by his rope, LONGHORN CAFE OPEN ALL NIGHT. Then a green peeling dinosaur, a Tyrannosaurus rex reaching out toward the road with DINO GAS painted in red on its side, a little sign that reads 8 MILES clutched in one claw.

Now it's dark, the lights of Evanston ahead of us, a few trailers on the outskirts of town barely discernible under the single light on the single pole, a feedlot filled with cattle, only their packed brown backs visible in the dim light, the stench so strong it wakes Ahna.

"Christ, what's that stink?"

"Cattle. We're just coming into Evanston."

She pulls her hair back, sits up. We're on the main
street, neon lights of motels, bars, the first block dom-
inated by a green dinosaur that towers over gas pumps,
lit by floodlights at its base, giving it the kind of gro-
tesque appearance you get when you hold a flashlight
under your chin.

CHAPTER 21

This time it's a Motel 6, one of those sterile buildings with a hole-in-the-wall clerk's desk behind glass and no pictures on the walls. It doesn't take long to settle Lucy into bed. There's a double and a single, and Lucy and Ahna share the double. Ahna is solicitous, washes out Lucy's underwear again, chews me out for not buying any this morning. I go down to the registration and buy apples and soft drinks from the vending machines.

When I get back, Lucy is asleep, Ahna has the television on, no sound, with the picture rolling every thirty seconds, an old movie. The TV set is bolted to a metal frame that juts out from the wall opposite the beds.

We cut the apples into pieces, pour the soft drinks into the thin plastic glasses from the bathroom, and sit on the edge of the beds facing each other. I hand Ahna the bag with the blouse in it.

"Here. I got this for you this morning."

"What is it?"

"Nothing. I saw it, and I figured I owed you something for taking care of Lucy the way you're doing."

She pulls out the blouse, fingers the sleeve, holds it across her chest.

"It's silk. Why?" She looks at me accusingly.

"Like I said, I felt I owed you something."

"This isn't a cheap nothing. What do you want?"

"Nothing. I did it on an impulse. You don't want it, put it back in the bag. Put it on Lucy."

She rises, goes into the bathroom and shuts the door. I can hear water running and a few minutes later she comes out wearing the blouse. The sleeves hang loosely from her shoulders.

"No weirdness?" she asks, pirouetting as if modeling the blouse.

"No weirdness," I reply.

She sits down next to me.

"Sometimes Lucy calls you Jack, sometimes she calls you Robert. Why?"

"She forgets."

"A couple of times today she called me Lucy."

She smells of motel soap and her musk perfume.

"Time for bed," I say. "It's been a long day."

She reaches over to the table and picks up the key to the room. "I'm going out. Look for a beer. I'm not tired yet." She rises and takes her purse. Then, without saying good-bye or see you later, she leaves the room, closing the door without looking back. The TV continues to roll and the mouths of the grainy figures move, but no sound comes.

I fall asleep almost immediately. It's after midnight when I wake with a start, sit bolt upright in bed, as if awakened by a loud noise, but it's only the door of the next room slamming shut, then muted voices from the other side of the wall, like the voices of the man and woman upstairs from my apartment. The TV is still rolling and Lucy is alone in her bed. No Ahna. I lie there for a while, trying to go back to sleep, but the people in the next room continue to talk, and finally I pull on my pants and shirt, check Lucy to make sure she's all right, and quietly step out onto the cement walkway that fronts the room. It's only after I close the door that I remember Ahna has the key and I walk quickly down to the registration and get a second one from the pimply-faced guy behind the glass window. The clock behind him says one A.M.

Ahna has to be within walking distance, and I set off to find her. Maybe have a drink, walk back to the motel with her.

There's not much along this street and it's easy to spot the bar a few blocks along. It's a low cement-block building surrounded on three sides by parking lot, a red neon line running along the front edge of the flat roof. When I open the door, I'm met by a continuous thump of sound. An imitation Eddie Van Halen stands on a low platform at the end of the room. He's bad, really bad, but the noise of his guitar reverberates through a portable sound system that makes up for its lack of quality with sheer, unadulterated volume. It's turned up so high that it fuzzes on every note like the sliding of thumb calluses on steel strings. The thrumming beat pulses immediately inside the reptile core of my brain, not really music, just sound, heavy and insistent. There is the smell of sweat and beer and cigarette smoke and even the trace of sweetish marijuana on the edge of the air.

I can't see much from just inside the door—mostly heads and shoulders jammed tightly, talking to each other in shouts above the music, their bodies unconsciously moving to the beat of the guitar, the backs of the heads to me and over their shoulders I can see into the room—smaller bobbing heads of a small group that must be dancing to the beat that presses my heart, makes it seem huge, ready to explode.

And I see Ahna, her hair flying, boogeying opposite, not two feet from this big redneck with a baseball cap, appearing, disappearing as she moves, the guy holding a beer in his upraised hand, a dumb shit-eating grin on his face, the kind you get when you're half bombed. I shoulder my way through to get closer, "Excuse me, excuse me," but nobody seems to notice, they just shout past my face.

Close enough to see her better now, she moves

with a wild abandon, the blouse sliding loosely on her shoulders, her hair obscuring her face. When she throws her head back, I can see her face glistening with sweat. She throws her shoulders back and twists them, her nipples tight against the shiny silk, and the redneck leans forward like he's going to bite one of them, his teeth bared like a dog's teeth.

He's got a pink baby face, puffy, with a neck that fills the collar of his faded blue T-shirt. Despite the puffiness of his face, he's not fat. He's got a beer belly, but it's powerful, like a sausage packed tight in the skin of his shirt. He moves clumsily. If this were L.A., I'd say sheetrocker or roofer.

"We've got to get up early tomorrow," I shout.

She stops moving her head to focus on me. "What's this *we* stuff?"

The cowboy looks pissed.

"Get yourself a beer," she says. The imitation Van Halen whacks off a last mind-jelling chord and takes a break. Ahna pulls her hair back and lifts it off her neck. She pulls it with both hands, stretching her face, the smooth wetness of her skin shining in the smoking light. For a moment it's the face of Egyptian sculpture, the high cheekbones, smooth-browed, nose in stone, the kind of woman who could lead the soldiers bare-breasted, riding above the dust and clouds of bluebottle flies.

"Who's watching the old lady?"

"She's asleep. You gonna stay here long?"

"Maybe," she says, pulling her blouse away from her chest and blowing down the hot wet skin.

The cowboy gets restless.

"C'mon, baby, you need a beer." He takes her by the wrist.

"Hey, wait a minute," I say.

"You got some objetsons." He can probably say "objections" when he's sober. I'm not dumb. This is the kind of guy who blows holes in old refrigerators at the end of the county road with heavy duty weapons.

"No."

"You belong to him?" he says to Ahna.

"I don't belong to *anyone*," she says, removing his hand from her wrist. She takes his beer from him and tips it, finishing it off.

CHAPTER 22

I hang around the edge of the crowd for a while watching for her and then I go out into the parking lot. The air burns, it's so clean, and I walk aimlessly up the street until a passing police car slows to look at me, and I head back toward the motel.

Passing the bar, I look inside, but the crowd has thinned, the band is gone, and Ahna is no longer there. Probably back at the motel.

Outside, for some reason, I notice the pickup truck in the parking lot against the wall of the building next door. It's by itself, backed against the brick, no other cars near it. It's jacked up on big tires, shocks that hold the body up so that the hood is almost level with my head. There's a square bulkiness to it, an ominous heaviness, poised and muscled. And there's two people in it. I wouldn't have thought anything about it, but one of them resembles, in some faint outline, Ahna, and I sidle along the bar in the shadow.

I want to see if it's her, and I want badly to see that it's not her. Close enough to make out the two heads, the guy is the same one she danced with and he's sitting in the middle of the seat facing the hood, and she's facing him. She's got to be sitting on his lap. His head is thrown back against the rear window of the cab and his eyes are closed. My eyes are cat's eyes now and they're gathering light from the streetlights and the moon and the starlight, intensifying the light so I can see his closed eyes and her shiny blouse. She's bouncing up and down, rhythmically, her hands braced on his shoulders, moving faster, pausing to flip her head so her hair comes out of her face, but her back is to me and I can't see any more than the mane of hair and the slick shimmer of the blouse and her hands and the corner of his face as he sinks lower.

Christ! Right here in the goddammed parking lot on the seat of his goddammed redneck muscle truck, and I think about finding a rock and throwing it at the windshield.

But I don't. Instead I go back inside the bar and buy a six-pack of beer and go back to the motel.

The buzz of the sign at the entrance to the motel is loud. The wind has died. The walkway with its intermittent doorways is lit by naked yellow bulbs. Another room that smells of motel. The half-open venetian blinds let in enough light to give shape to the beds, the lump under the covers that is Lucy, the chair by the door. I bend over Lucy. She still sleeps, faceup, mouth open, her breath coming in little rasps.

I strip to my shorts and sit on the bed opposite, crack open a beer. From here I can see through the slats of the half-drawn blinds to the yellowed walkway and the hoods of cars drawn up in front of the rooms. Somewhere in the motel there is a flush or the sound of water turned on, then off. It comes in a rush in the pipes in the wall behind my head.

I feel certain Ahna won't come back. I want Ahna to come back. Not just to care for Lucy. Christ, this is so screwed up I can't believe it. By now they're looking for Lucy. They've got to be. I've got to be absolutely duck-brained stupid to be here, and what I should do is stow Lucy Boomer in the car and drive like a maniac back to L.A. and get my act together.

"Get my act together." The words are out loud in the air, floating in front of me, and I suck on the beer until the can is empty. Talking to myself in a motel room that smells like a damp ashtray in a town full of redneck cowboys, waiting for some hippie nympho to come wandering in out of the night.

She'll probably spend the night with the cowboy. Wearing the blouse that I gave her. Which she didn't ask for.

I'm going to pound down this whole goddamn six-pack and go to sleep, and when it's light I'm going to sort out whatever the hell I'm doing because in the daylight it's easier to see a map.

South of here there's some mountains called the Cortez Mountains. I remember seeing them when I looked at the map at the last rest stop before we saw the dogs in the field. Why would anybody name some mountains in Wyoming after Cortez? Some lost historian? Ponce de Leon wasn't looking for the Fountain of Youth when he went up through Florida. No way, baby. He was looking for the pot of gold, just like me. His buddies, Cortez and Pizarro, they lucked into big bucks, but poor old Ponce, he had nothing but a little piss-ant island, so he went north to find *his* fortune. I imagine he spent a few nights in motels wondering what the hell *he* was doing.

Mary Lea and I went to Florida once. The car crapped out on a little road in the swamps that was a solid black line on the map but turned out to be a gravel road that turned into sand and big swales of water and then the car died. We walked about a mile to the main highway, nothing but clouds of mosquitoes swarming around us, frogs along the road hidden in swampy pools of greasy gray water; the frogs sounded like old men clearing their throats, and when we took shelter from a cloudburst under some low trees, there was a lizard on the tree trunk, a little gray thing doing jerky push-ups. And a big fleshy disc appeared at the base of his throat, crimson, like a slice of brilliant ruby the size of a quarter, a round blade that extended, then disappeared. Some sort of sexual attractor, I supposed. Jacking off there for another lizard I couldn't see, the rain coming down as warm as the air around us. Mary Lea's legs were a solid mass of red welts, and I expected her to cry, but she didn't, just marched through the rain and the ankle-deep pools until we got to the highway where a couple in a van on their way to the coast picked us up.

Nobody picked Ponce up. He marched all the way to Georgia, turned left, and died on the banks of the Mississippi. Lucy wants to die in Iowa. I felt like I was dead in L.A. High drama when you're starting to feel really drunk, which is what I'm starting to feel right now.

Headlights sweep across the blinds and I wait, but there's only the crunch of tires on gravel, a door slams, low voices, no Ahna. No more Ahna. My head's beginning to ache. Maybe I should go in the bathroom and stick a finger down my throat and puke.

I wake up when she comes back to the motel. I hear this fumbling at the door and I sit up, but I'm not in such good shape myself, so it's a few moments before I realize it's Ahna. Finally, she gets the door open. First she goes to the bathroom and throws up. I wonder if Lucy is awake and can hear the abrupt barking and coughing and the rush of the toilet's flush. The sweetish smell of vomit comes through the half-open bathroom door, and there's a thump as she tries to rise and falls against something.

Then Ahna comes out, momentarily framed by the light from the bathroom, pulling at her blouse, trying to shed it as she crosses toward the bed where Lucy lies. I'm afraid that she's forgotten Lucy is in it, and she'll collapse on the little body that barely makes a lump in the covers. I'm just about to say something, but Ahna sort of kneels at the edge of the bed, as if she were sliding into a kind of genuflection, lifts the sheet and crawls up under it. She's almost immediately asleep, one arm trailing from the bed, touching the floor, the blouse bunched in a pool at her wrist, illuminated by the light still spilling from the open bathroom door.

CHAPTER 23

When I go to the bathroom this morning, it's a mess.
There's vomit spattered on the seat of the toilet and
little bits of stuff floating in the bowl. I flush the toilet
several times and wipe the seat and rim with a towel. I
stand in the shower a long time, letting the water run
on the back of my neck, hoping it will ease my headache, open my mouth under the shower and let the
water flood in, drink and spit out again and again. When
I go out into the room wiping myself with a towel,
Ahna is lying on her side facing me, holding her hair
away from her face. She looks terrible. I pull my pants
on and sit on the edge of the bed facing her.

"You look like shit," I say.

She doesn't respond.

"So where were you?"

"None of your goddamn business." Her voice isn't
hostile, just matter-of-fact. Neither of us says anything
more about last night. She goes into the bathroom and

I hear the shower flooding her, too, and then she comes out, her hair wrapped in a towel like a huge turban, and she takes care of Lucy.

What I mean is she washes Lucy with a washcloth, pats her dry, dresses her, all with a gentle patience, as if she's cared for an old person before, speaking softly to her as she raises Lucy's thin shoulders to slip the blouse on, lifting her hips to put on the skirt.

When she's finished, I carry Lucy to the car. Ahna says nothing to me. She rubs the towel vigorously in her hair and fishes a brush out of her bag to comb out the wet tangles while we drive off in search of a place to have breakfast.

I find a McDonald's and we eat dry little egg sandwiches and drink hot coffee in the car. Lucy asks Ahna to sit in the back seat with her, and by the time we're an hour out of Evanston, their heads are close together, Lucy's on Ahna's shoulder like a child with its mother, only this strange reversal has the old woman playing the child's role. In the rearview mirror I can see Lucy talking, her lips moving, and Ahna is either listening with her eyes closed or sleeping. Considering the shape she was in this morning, I suspect Lucy might as well be talking to a rock, but she keeps her lips moving next to Ahna's ear.

We're just outside of Green River when the noise begins to get louder. It started yesterday, a quiet whine that comes from under the car. At first I thought it was tire noise, but it's steadily grown louder this morning and I know it's the transmission.

Green River. There was a photograph in our family album of my father in Green River. He was standing next to a locomotive, my grandmother next to him, her hand on his shoulder. What used to strike me as a child was the fact that she was taller than he was. I found it hard to reconcile my tiny grandmother with the middle-aged man I always remembered as my father. Next to them was a black porter in his black suit, shiny-billed porter's cap, holding a step stool. The bottom of the photograph was white, the steam from the locomotive swirling in the foreground. The photograph was taken by my grandfather, and on the back in my grandmother's tiny, spidery handwriting was written, "Edwin, age 10 in Green River Wyoming on our way West."

The transmission howls like a crazed wolf. Borrowing from Wordsworth there. Or did he say the crazed ice howled like a transmission? No matter, it's this steady high-pitched whine in high gear that rises and falls when I put pressure on the gas or release it. I'm growing accustomed to it. It's sort of comforting, a humming that accompanies us like a banshee that's come along for the ride. But it means that we've got to get it fixed, if it's fixable, or the odyssey has come to an end.

The noise is loud enough to bring Ahna back to life.

"What's that noise?"

"I think it's the transmission."

"You going to get it fixed?"

"If I have enough money. Otherwise the ride's over."

"So what are you going to do?"

We're traveling through the tree-shaded streets of Green River and I'm looking for a gas station with a mechanic. I find one on a side street right on the edge of town with a cluttered mechanic's bay, lots of old hulks and oil drums outside, and a young guy who comes out wiping his hands on an oily rag. He listens to my description, rides around the block with us and says he can fix it.

"Maybe a hundred, hundred and a half," he says laconically.

"How long will it take?"

"You want it *now?*" he asks. He gestures to a truck with its hood up. "I got to finish that. Maybe I could get to you by noon. Have you outta here by three. I assume it's cash." He talks to me but he keeps looking over the back of his seat at Ahna, lifting his baseball cap with one hand, running his grease-blackened fingers through his hair with the other.

Ahna and Lucy stay in the car. I go off to find some cold drinks since it's heating up. When I get back, the mechanic is deep in the bowels of the truck.

The station is at the edge of town, and behind the

building is an oil-stained parking lot, a fence, then rail-road tracks and open fields. Beyond the station, across the tracks, across the field stubble, there is a heron. It startles me because I've always associated herons with the coast. The heron moves like a marionette, only the stilted legs moving, the body attached to them stiff, while the leg lifts at the joint, the body balances on one leg impossibly, and then the leg is lowered by the string I cannot see.

Audubon taught himself to draw birds. As a child in the south of France he drew the carcasses that lay in rows in the street market of Nantes. Later he complained that his drawings looked dead. Dead birds with sticks for legs, he said. The heron must have been an easy bird to draw; body the color of gun metal against the yellow stubble, stick legs lifting in slow motion, bending at the silly joints. This old man of a bird stiff-legs across the field, picking his way, head cocked to one side, moving so slowly that only by squinting my eyes and matching him with a fence post on the far side of the field do I see that he is moving from left to right.

A plastic cup is lodged in the weeds at my feet, and a sun-bleached beer can. The more I look, the more I see: some brittle plastic sheeting blown against the barbed wire fence, and above that, hanging on the barbed wire, is what appears to be a ragged towel, but it has what looks like a grinning face near one corner.

I pick my way through the weeds to get a closer

look. It's not a towel, it's an animal. Was an animal. The carcass of a coyote has been hung on the fence by someone, the barbs hooked through the skin. It's been here a long time, stiff, dehydrated, windworn, so that the outline of the creature is long gone. The skull, not much bigger than my bunched fist, covered with gray fuzz and tufts of brownish hair, stares blindly through holes where eyes once were. There is no smell of decay, only the hot weed and tar smell of the asphalt.

They hang crows on fences, too. I saw some on the fence of the mission garden in San Juan Bautista, their feet hooked into the barbs, wings hanging downward, feathers dried and dull in the sun. The wingtip feathers spread out like fingers on dead hands. As if a live crow or coyote, seeing its dead cousin tacked up there is going to say, "Shee-it, these guys mean it," and go the other way. Sort of like nailing muggers up on trees in parks, or spiking the body of a thief above the apartment door where it, too, dries in the sun until the eyes are gone.

The Greeks thought the soul crawled off the tongue and turned into dust. I'm reminded of the coyotes in Claremont and the banker's wife in her rich house above the tract houses. Her house smelled of leather and wax and cut flowers. She never did housework. Once, the Mexican maid came out on the deck by mistake when I was there one afternoon. It scared the hell out of me, but the banker's wife said, "Don't worry, she can't speak any English." And the maid acted like two naked bodies drying in the sun were the most natural things in the world. Like we were dogs sunning ourselves. She shook the mop and went inside and I never saw her again.

I unhook the coyote skin from the fence. It's hard and pieces break off in my hands when I pull it away from the barbs. I sail it out into the field beyond the fence. I have no idea why. My hands smell like dust.

CHAPTER 24

By four the car is fixed. I count out a hundred and sixty bucks in twenties and feel lucky. It's left a sizable dent in my cash, but at least we're on the road again. I want to get to Cheyenne tonight, and it's another six hours of driving. Lucy wants to sit in the front, and we bundle her in between the two of us. Ahna feels okay now. Alongside the highway a train snakes past us, and Ahna talks animatedly about a guy she dated once who worked for the railroad and how he'd sneak her aboard the engine. She starts to describe how they'd make it in the cab while the train was thundering along, and it's embarrassing with Lucy there. I try to change the subject but then I see that Lucy is hanging on every word, her fingers entwined in Ahna's long hair, so I just look straight ahead and drive.

Then Lucy is telling Ahna something and I can't hear it.

"What's she saying?"

"She's telling me about some guy she went out with when she was my age. She calls him W."

"She calls him what?"

"W. Just the letter. His initial, I guess."

And Lucy tells Ahna her story, and Ahna repeats each line for me, like a translator.

Lucy's story: "It was just after the war started." "Which war?" Ahna asks me. "If she was in her twenties," I say, "it was the First World War." "They were coming east in trains, all these young men, and when they came through Washington we went down to the station to wave to them. W. had to go, and I loved going with him. There were bands and they played brassy songs and the flags were everywhere. It was like a great party and they all seemed so handsome. They filled the windows of the trains and they hung out the doors, their tight brown tunics and tight leggings showing off their muscled bodies, and they were like electricity filling me. I could picture where they'd come from, Iowa and Nebraska and even California, and they were off to France and great adventure, and I envied them. I had no idea they were going off to get butchered, and they didn't either, but W. knew what was happening. He was a calculating bastard."

She looks at me for the first time and touches my arm. "I thought I'd live forever, Robert," she says.

"Lucy, I'm not Robert, I'm Jack."

Ahna watches me quizzically. We plunge ahead, the headlights making a cone of yellow ahead of us, insects suddenly flashing into the windshield. Then she asks, "Who was Robert?"

"Somebody she's got me confused with."

"No," she says, not accepting my vague answer. "Who was he?"

"Her brother."

"What happened to him?"

"I don't know. I suppose he's dead. He was older."

"Do you look like him?"

"I don't know."

"You don't know much, do you?"

"Less every day."

"Jesus, you're impossible!" She pulls Lucy down into her lap, cradling her, stroking her wispy hair.

I feel as if the car has ceased to move—that the outside world is rushing past, like those moments in the cowboy films where the wagon spokes freeze in one place yet the chase thunders on. The lights of a low house appear, slide past. Trucks with dozens of red and yellow lights appear, grow larger, rocket past us. Soon we'll be in Cheyenne. The wind whistles shrilly at the window next to me, and I crank hard at the handle, trying to force the glass tight enough to kill the noise. It won't stop, so I crack the window open a bit and the whistle is replaced by a rush of cold night air. Ahna pulls Lucy's blanket around both of them.

RUSSELL HILL

"Who do you suppose W. was?" she says. Her words are almost lost in the wind noise.

I'm about to say "Woodrow," but I stop myself. It's too complicated to explain who Lucy is.

"I don't know."

More lights now. The outskirts of Cheyenne. I pull into the first motel that has a vacancy sign.

121

CHAPTER 25

Another late night meal. Lucy is asleep and Ahna and I sit on opposite sides of the bedside nightstand. She's draped a towel over the lamp to soften the light. The rest of the room is in darkness. We eat hamburgers and drink beer like two conspirators, Ahna wrapped in a blanket, her feet tucked under her on the bed, me sitting on the other bed facing her.

Ahna's face is softer in this light. Her teeth are straight, too perfect to be naturally that way. Someone, somewhere, had them straightened, but there's a tiny chip out of the corner of one front tooth. She's washed her hair again tonight and wrapped it in a towel. Her forehead is high, accentuated by the tightly wrapped turban, and her skin is polished, shining in the muted light.

"She's a neat old lady, Jack," Ahna says between bites. "She told me the wildest stories all morning long."

"I thought you were asleep."

"I was, sort of, but I could hear her voice the whole time. It was like I was wearing earphones or something."

"What did she tell you?"

"All kinds of stuff. Like she lived in this huge white house with this guy who was already married. I guess he was famous or something. Anyway, they went on safari to Africa, shot all kinds of things, lions, zebras, rhinos, you name it. She said she was really a good shot. I think it was the same Teddy guy who rode his horse up on the porch. Remember him?"

"Probably. What else did she say?"

She finishes her burger and wipes the corners of her mouth with a paper napkin.

"It's hard to remember. Tents and lanterns and weird coughing animal noises at night. It's strange. It was like I could hear the noises and smell the stuff she was talking about. You know what I mean?"

I nod.

"And sex. Jack, she talks about these guys like she's twenty years old."

"What does she say?"

"Hey, Jack, you're going to have to get off some other way than listening to me tell you about her conquests." She grins at me. Her eyes have the same brown flecks as Lucy's.

There's a sudden bang and the room shudders.

We're both startled, and then I realize it's the wind. It's blowing hard outside, and a door or something has slammed in a quick, violent gust.

It occurs to me that all over Cheyenne others have been startled. At this moment people are making love, watching television, someone is replacing a flat tire in the windy darkness along an unnamed road. Dogs in back alleys pause, ears alert, hair rising on their backs. And even the sleeping ones pause, uneasy for a moment in their dreams when the wind shakes the house. I reach across through the light and touch Ahna's neck at the base of her throat, pressing with my fingers at the ridge of bone. It's a reflex action, something I don't think about until I've done it, and just as quickly I withdraw my hand.

She smiles. "You're kind of a nice guy, Jack. Most guys wouldn't want to take an old lady halfway across the country."

She unwraps the blanket from around her shoulders and slides under the covers next to Lucy. For a quick moment she's naked in the half light and I want to touch her again. But she turns her back, pulling herself close to Lucy and murmurs, "Good night."

CHAPTER 26

This morning Ahna comes out of the bathroom and I want to hold her. I reach out, put my hand on her shoulder and she does not draw away. I put my hand on the back of her head and draw her to me. She's dried her hair with a towel but it's still wet and I can feel her skull, like the skull of a small animal cupped in my palm. She opens her mouth and her tongue is in my mouth. I smell her wet hair and feel the softness of her lips. Her teeth touch mine. Tongues. The word is a thick and soft and insistent muscle that pushes, speaks even when there's no noise. Her eyes are open but they look beyond me into someone or something else, through my forehead.

"What was that all about?" she asks, pulling back, picking the towel off the bed, rubbing her hair with it, her voice muffled as she buries her head. Her voice is matter-of-fact.

"Sorry, it was an impulse."

"Don't be sorry," she says.

"No weirdness," I say, trying to reassure her.

But she only tips her head forward until the hair cascades down, rubbing it with the towel, and says, "I've met guys a lot more weird than you, Jack. Or Robert." She raises her head to look at me. "How much farther to where you're taking Lucy?"

"Another day or so. Today we cross Nebraska. Tomorrow we're in Iowa."

And Nebraska seems endless. We're off early, and I-80 goes on straight for hours. I stop twice for gas and food. It feels like I could put a brick on the accelerator and go to sleep and the car would just keep on going.

Ahna dozes in the back with Lucy, and the monotony of the interstate gets to me by early afternoon. Ahna is asleep. Her head leans against the window, the hot air blowing her hair about her face. My eyes ache from the continuous shine of the concrete. I rub saliva onto the lids of my eyes with my fingers, let the wind evaporate it into sudden coolness in an attempt to keep awake. In the back seat Lucy, too, is asleep, the damp towel we spread on her to keep her cool now dried and blown into a corner of the seat.

Finally, afraid I'll drift off, I ease the car onto the shoulder near a shallow draw, where a tree provides some shade, and stop. The heat rises from the highway in shimmering waves, and I can see for miles across the undulating cornfields. The wash runs through a low concrete bridge under the freeway. In the stillness of the fields little scree! scree! sounds come as birds dart up from beneath the bridge. I walk to the edge and look down. The birds pop up singly, erratically, suddenly rising and corkscrewing into the air. There is no other sound except for their insistent squeaks.

A slight, hot wind stirs the corn and it rustles. A grasshopper starts up from the weeds at my feet, cracking loudly. The air is heavy and smells like the earth. It's as if I'm in the center of the world, the car behind me in the shade, abandoned, and I am the tallest thing there is. In L.A. things wore out and they got replaced. Here, things die and then grow again. I'm surrounded by the smell of stuff growing. Corn, pigs, cows, families, pickup trucks. Lucy is drawn to it, and I'm sucked along in the slipstream, and I don't know where Ahna fits into this. It's as if Lucy is accelerating into Iowa and I'm just hanging onto the steering wheel as best I can.

The two of them are still asleep when I come back to the car, although it's hard to tell with Lucy whether she's sleeping or she's just got her body in neutral and she's taking in what goes on around her.

Half an hour later Ahna and Lucy are awake. I ask Lucy if the landscape looks familiar. She asks where we are.

"Nebraska. We're getting close to Grand Island."

Ahna helps her to sit erect so she can look out the window. She stares for a long time. She says something but I can't make out what it is, and I roll up the window to stop the noise of the wind. She looks toward me and I can see her bony face in the rearview mirror, the skin of her forehead shiny and translucent.

"After they cut the corn you can see a long way," Lucy says. "Sometimes it's as if you can see the edge of the earth." She looks again out the window. Then she turns to Ahna. "Did you ever have a dog?"

Ahna shakes her head, no.

"My father had a three-legged hunting dog," Lucy says. "Skippy. One of his legs was cut off by a mower. The long-bladed kind that horses drew." Her voice goes up as if she's questioning, and I nod my head to show I understand what she means. She continues, "They start on the edge of the field and go 'round and 'round until the unmowed part gets smaller and smaller in the center and rabbits and pheasants and mice and whatever else lives in the wheat go to the center and pretty soon the whole patch is just alive."

She pauses again. It's hard to hear above the noise of the car. Maybe she's drifted off.

"Go on, Lucy. What happened?"

Her voice comes again, stronger. "That's when father would stop the horses and sic Skippy in there and let him flush them out, and sometimes Robert and Howard and Earl would have their shotguns and they would shoot whatever came out. Only Skippy got too excited. He just leaped in before the horses stopped and that's how he lost the leg. He still hunted on three legs. When he got to running, you could hardly tell there wasn't a leg there."

"Did you call him Skippy because he only had three legs?" I ask.

"No. Father said he was a blue dog. When he got old he got blind in one eye. It looked like a cloudy blue marble."

She pauses again. There's a childlike quality even though it's still Lucy's barely audible voice. I look in the rearview mirror to see if she's still with us. Her gaunt face is resolute, and her eyes seem to look straight at me and past, through the mirror at something far off down the road, and then she focuses on me as if seeing me for the first time.

"Do you hunt, Jack?" she asks the mirror.

"No."

"I used to see Robert and Skippy go off to hunt geese in November. Robert carried an old sheet with him. There would be a few inches of snow in the fields, and some corn stubble showing through. Robert would lie on the ground with the sheet over Skippy and him so the geese couldn't see them. When it got near dark, I'd go to the gate and wait for them. It was cold. I'd see the two of them coming across the field. Robert always had geese. When they came across the farmyard, they always looked so alone."

She focuses on me again.

"It was like there wasn't anybody or anything else in the world except them."

I look away at the road, then glance back. Her eyes are still fixed on me.

"You ever kill anything, Jack?" She closes her eyes, and I look again at the road. The light is going now, the cornfields darkening, rushing past on either side. It's strange. Here I am, Southern California boy, never saw an Iowa field in November, I only know hot brown hills and flat beaches, but I can see the young man and the dog as clearly as if I were there.

CHAPTER 27

I swing north on Highway 30 out of Grand Island and angle toward Iowa. Just at dark we cross the Missouri River and finally we're in Iowa, but Lucy is asleep or out of it so there's no celebration. I've got exactly $258 left, we need to stop for the night, I've got four days, at least, back to L.A., and there's no way I can take Ahna to Chicago.

For $28 I get a room in an old hotel near the bus depot in Denison, worn carpet, faded drapes, and I can smell the old salesmen who used to stay here. But there's a back stairwell, so I can carry Lucy up without a lot of attention, and the price is right. The room looks out over the highway which is the main street through town.

Then there's the search for dinner. Lucy wants McDonald's burgers when she wakes up—she's lived on those since the second day. No luck in finding any, but I do find a Dairy Queen still open, buy burgers and fries, and Ahna and I sit on Lucy's bed and eat from the bag, wiping greasy fingers on the edges of the thin gray sheet.

It's awkwardly quiet. I tell Lucy we're in Iowa, but she doesn't seem to respond. Ahna keeps silent and sits close to Lucy, helping her to eat.

Then we're finished and I watch Ahna tend to Lucy, stripping her, washing her with a warm washcloth, brushing her hair.

While Ahna is in the bathroom I undress and get into the other bed, but I lie, like Lucy, flat on my back, hands at my sides, listening to the little noises in the bathroom, Ahna taking a pee, the flush of the toilet, the water in the basin running. Then the door opens and she comes out.

She walks on her toes, lifting herself up on the balls of her feet, her heels never seeming to touch the floor. She's wearing just the silk blouse, it's open, and I can see the dark triangle at the base of her belly. She moves slowly to the window, pensively, as if she's thinking about someplace far off, and she looks out. The material of the blouse shimmers, catching little flashes of light, maybe cars going by on the street below, and she draws the curtains. The room is nearly dark now, the light from the streetlights leaking in around the cheap drapes. She comes to the bed where I am, puts one knee on the end and stretches out her hands on both sides of my legs. Her breasts droop and she looks like a spider inside a silken tent, like the cocoons that the tent caterpillars make high in the oak trees, gray gossamer things with the branches like her elbows, all sharp and angled where they stretch the cocoon. And she's over me, on her hands and knees, still spiderlike, the blouse making this dark cave so that I can only see the outline of her drooping breasts and the roundness of her belly and her hair, hanging down around her head, wild and frizzy. And I forget about Lucy in the bed opposite, forget about everything except that she's on top of me, and then I'm on top of her and she's wrapped around me and then it's over—except that she lies there on her back, her hands pressed to the sides of her head, pressing her palms to her temples as if her head is splitting in two and she's holding it together and her face looks like she's in terrible pain.

"You all right?" I ask.

"Shut up," through gritted teeth. Then, "I hear water running over stones."

And she raises her hips and draws me down again.

When I awake Ahna is beside me on her back, arms at her sides in the Lucy position. She's asleep, or at least I think she is, since she's breathing slowly, mouth open, eyes closed.

Her breasts are flat against her chest, and I lean toward her, touch the nipple of one with my tongue, run my lips across it until it starts to swell.

Ahna stirs.

I run my hand down her leg, touch the inside of her thigh.

"What are you doing?" Sleepy voice.

"Touching you."

"Not now," she says. "I have to get back to my room. What time is it?" Her voice is disembodied, as if she's speaking from a long distance.

Her hands cross on her stomach.

"Ain't no room except this one." And then I add, "Are you awake?"

She turns her head to look at me. She blinks, as if to clear her vision. "I was having a dream," she says.

"A good one?"

"I have to pee," she says, and swings her legs over the side of the bed.

The door to the bathroom half closes and I look toward Lucy, who lies, too, on her back, arms at her sides.

At that moment there is a shriek from the bathroom. I leap out of bed, yank the door open. Ahna stands in front of the sink, looking in the mirror, rubbing furiously at the side of her stomach.

She turns, stretching the skin of her belly tight.

"Jesus Christ!" she screams. "Look at this!"

"Look at what?"

"This goddamn scar! I never had a goddamn scar. She's given it to me!"

"Ahna, what the hell are you talking about? You haven't got any scar." Her belly is pink where she's rubbed it, but it's smooth, not a mark on it.

"What do you call this?" But now her voice is smaller, scared. She picks at the skin of her belly, kneading it, as if she's actually got a scar welt between her fingers. She pushes past me, lunges toward Lucy's bed and tears the sheets off.

"It's smaller! Look, her goddamn appendectomy scar is smaller." She points to a thin red line on Lucy's skin. "This crazy old woman is giving me her scar!"

"Ahna, you don't have a scar. People don't give other people their scars."

Her hair hangs down over her face, obscuring it as she picks at herself. There's a big red patch now where she's frantically rubbing at her skin. I half expect her to throw back her head, fling her hair back and laugh at the joke, but it's apparently no joke. Whatever's happened to her, she believes she has a scar. I try again to reassure her.

"Ahna, you don't have a scar. Believe me." I reach out, put my hand on her belly, but she slaps it away.

"Her scar was bigger." Her voice is hard, angry now. She turns to Lucy, leans over, takes her by the shoulders and shakes her.

"Wake up you old bitch! What the hell are you doing to me?" Her hair hangs over Lucy's body, the cloud of hair connecting Ahna to Lucy.

"Hey, take it easy." I grab her from behind and pull her off. She's breathing hard.

Lucy's eyes are open. Her tiny naked body seems smaller now, the head bigger, as if it's grown in size.

Ahna jerks away from me.

"Jesus Christ!" Ahna examines her stomach, running her fingers up and down the side of it. Abruptly she goes into the bathroom and shuts the door.

I pull the covers back over Lucy who lies still, staring up at the ceiling. I bend over her.

"It's all right. Ahna's upset."

Lucy's voice floats up, ethereal, as if it comes not from her barely moving lips, but from around her, like the sound you hear when you hold a shell to your ear.

"Are we in Iowa, Robert?"

"Dammit, Lucy, I'm not Robert. I'm Jack. Remember? Jack, who's taking you to Iowa so you'll give him the diaries. Remember?"

The diaries. Joke's on me. I haven't thought about the damn diaries since we left L.A.

"Did you make love to her, Robert?"

"For God's sake, Lucy!"

"Did you?"

"None of your business."

I could swear she grins.

I have to dress her. She seems smaller, like the husk of something—as if, were I to dip her in water, she would dissolve, drift through my fingers like silk rotted by the sun. She feels Iowa, she says, and she asks for Ahna, but Ahna stays in the bathroom, the shower running until, finally, I bang on the door to ask if she's all right. No answer, but the water stops running, and when she comes out, her mouth is set and she won't speak.

There's nothing open in Denison except a café filled with big men in overalls hunched over coffee cups, so I drive until I find a store open in the next town, buy little boxes of cereal, and we eat them in the car, pouring milk into the little boxes. I have to feed Lucy. Ahna stares out the window.

It's nearly ten o'clock when Ahna turns to me and announces she wants to get out at the next town. I protest that we're in the middle of nowhere and there's no way she's going to get a ride.

"It doesn't matter," she says. "I've got to get away from her." She emphasizes the last word with a jerk of her head toward Lucy in the backseat.

"Why? I thought you liked her. She asked for you this morning, Ahna. She cares for you."

Ahna puts a hand on the dashboard as if to steady herself. "No," she says, "it's more than that. She's doing something to me. I'm like some kind of empty container that she's filling up, and that's not all. I remember things. She'll be talking and then she'll drift off like she does, but the story keeps on going in my head, just like it's *her* talking, only it's *my* voice. And remembering stuff that never happened to me."

"Like what?"

"God, it's so hard to sort out. What's hers and what's mine. She lived in this big white house."

"Not this big white house, Ahna. *The* White House."

"Which white house?"

"The one presidents live in."

"No." A beat. Eyes narrow. "Who is she, Jack?"

"She's Lucy Boomer."

"She's not related to you."

"No."

"Then how in hell did you end up with her?"

"I promised to take her to Iowa so she could die."

"She's dying, isn't she?"

"Yes."

"No, I mean right now, this very instant, a piece at a time. Only she's not really dying, Jack. She's becoming me. Or I'm becoming her. I don't know which."

"Look," I say. "Let's not get spooky. She's an old lady and she's dying and we're taking her home. That's all."

"Then explain this." She pulls her blouse up and grabs a handful of flesh with clenched fingers as if she's trying to give a fistful to me. "And explain how I remember fucking some three-hundred-pound dude I've never seen in this big white house I've never been in."

And I'm back in L.A. at the Huntington Library where Schofield is telling me about this old lady in Tarzana who was a secretary in the White House. It all seemed so simple four days ago. Take Lucy to Iowa, let her look around, come back, get the diaries. Now, this morning, crossing Iowa, it's lunatic. I've got a hippie girl who's fantasizing a scar, a dying old woman who calls me by her dead brother's name, and slightly more than two hundred bucks in my pocket. The only thing to do is press on. I can't just carry Lucy back into the nursing home and say, "Oh, gosh, were you looking for her?" Without Ahna's help I can't even get her back to Los Angeles.

All my life I have saved the past like some old man rolling bits of string into an immense ball; saved old photos, read the journals and diaries of others. Some people invent their own lives, others have their lives invented for them. I cannot tell if Lucy's past is all lies or if it is real but it no longer matters. There are things which are true for a moment and then some other truth is layered over them, like paintings on the same canvas, bits and pieces added until the original is hidden, only vaguely remembered, or to those who never saw the first scene, not there at all.

"Stay one more night," I plead with Ahna. "Tomorrow I'll buy you a ticket to Chicago. You can't leave us now."

She says nothing. By mid-afternoon I know she'll stay. She moves into the backseat with Lucy.

Just before Carroll we go through a town where

I'm startled to see buggies with horses tied to a railing around the square, and then I realize that they belong to Mennonites. Leaving town, we pass one of the square black buggies with a huge reflective orange triangle on the back, obviously put there to warn cars of the slow-moving buggy that is half on the pavement, half off, the horses moving steadily, heads down, bobbing in unison, a black-hatted, black-coated man driving. We pass several farms with no curtains in the windows, plain, unpainted, yet painstakingly neat, the only sign of life being the clothesline at one farm with dull colorless clothing hanging, a woman in a long dress gathering shirts and trousers into a basket at her feet.

At dusk we pass a barnyard where two men, bare-chested, shout and pull at the traces of two giant horses, trying to get them to back up. A woman stands at one side watching. The horses snort and one rears, tangling the traces while the men haul at it and shout it down. In the half light it seems as if time is a wall and we have driven by a half-open door, seen a flash of a parallel world on the other side. I want to call out to Lucy, tell her to look, but they are gone as quickly as they appeared. A half hour later, under the streetlights of the next town, passing the Dairy Queen ringed with cars and flickering moths, I feel as if those men and horses had never been there at all.

CHAPTER 28

The streets of Carroll are nearly deserted, storefronts, dark, yellow lights over a lot with tractors and farm equipment making them look slightly outer spacey. Ahna stares out the window and says nothing about getting out. Lucy sleeps, I think.

Suddenly Ahna says, "This is it!"

"This is what?"

"Where she comes from. Someplace around here."

I pull the car over to the curb. Ahna is still staring out the window. Nothing moves on the street.

"Did she tell you?" I ask

Ahna faces me. Her eyes are hollows in the darkness, her cheekbones highlighted by the streetlight.

"No, I don't know. I just feel it. Here." She jerks her head toward the street. "Don't ask me how I know it." Her voice is unsteady and she turns to look over the back of the seat at Lucy.

"Lucy," she says. "We're here."

Lucy doesn't respond. Ahna stretches over the

back of the seat, wipes Lucy's hair from her face, touches her cheek. "We're here, Lucy."

I can't see Lucy's face clearly, but I can hear the faint voice. "I know."

CHAPTER 29

The old hotel in Carroll is a lot like the motels we've been staying at. The interstate has Motel 6's and Holiday Inns, but when you get into these small towns, everything seems to have passed them by, and I feel like I'm in some sort of time warp when I get inside the room. Like somebody drove faster than me and left the same *National Geographic* beside the bed, hung the same print of a creek surrounded by autumn leaves above the bed, stretched the same worn nubby chenille bedspread across each of the beds.

There's no motel in Carroll, only this old brick three-story hotel on the main street, with narrow stale hallways and carpet with the flowers worn to the backing.

It's quiet in the room. Nobody says anything. Ahna cleans Lucy up, washes her underwear in the sink, hangs it over the back of a chair to dry. Lucy is tucked into bed, the covers up to her chin, looking like no more than a folding of covers, as if someone had care-lessly made the bed and left a long fold under the bed-spread where her thin body lies.

I ask Ahna again how she knows this is where Lucy was born, but she just says again that she knows it is, don't ask any more goddamn questions, I don't know how the hell I know, and she disappears into the bathroom. I hear water running for a long time and realize she's filling the tub.

When Ahna comes out of the bathroom, she's dressed, her hair still damp, and she bends to kiss Lucy on the forehead and murmur something to her before she leaves. No word for me. No good-bye. She closes the door and the room is silent. I lie there for a while listening to the hotel noises, the old ice machine at the end of the hallway clunking and occasionally releasing a crash of cubes, the faint voice of a television set. There is a hum, a motor or a generator, or maybe it's a truck engine outside. There's a sharp erratic clicking that comes and goes, and when I locate it, it's an insect banging against the shade of the lamp next to Lucy's bed. It, too, falls silent.

Lucy's breathing comes shallowly, little sips of air. I try again to imagine what she must have looked like when she was younger. And I can't. In fact, I have a hard time remembering what she was like in the nursing home in Tarzana. Is she more frail now? Is she smaller?

Lucy's eyes are open and she's making little gasping noises. Her eyes are bright, and they dart from side to side.

"Lucy," I ask, "you all right?"

Her lips move but I hear no sound. I move to the edge of her bed and sit on it, smoothing her wispy hair back from her forehead. Her head is small, as if I'm cupping something the size of a coconut in my fingers, but slick, burnished, the skin drawn tight over the skull, and it strikes me how small our skulls are.

Long ago, when I was a teacher in a junior college in California, I used a skull to talk about how historians could reconstruct the lives of long-dead people, discover how they died, how the marks on the skull told us it was a child who died in a fall, or a warrior who had been brained by a stone axe. Lucy's forehead feels like that skull, but it's warm, a parchment of skin and flesh keeping it alive.

And I remember Mary Lea once, her leaning against the doorjamb of the study in a friend's house, both of us watching outselves in the long mirror on the opposite wall, watching my blind hands unbutton her blouse, somewhere else in the house children calling out, a party going on, looking at the mirror as if it were a film, the hands of someone else slipping inside the blouse, the face of a woman I no longer knew watching intently, mouth slightly open.

Lucy is trying to talk again. I bend to hear, putting my ear next to her lips.

"Do something, Jack," she says.

"Do what, Lucy? What can I do?" My hand is still cupped around her head, and I can feel her jaw moving.

"Do something unspeakable, Jack," she says, and there's an urgency in her voice, each word coming in a whisper of spit.

"What do you mean?"

She hisses the words: "Take off your clothes and run naked through the streets. Don't wait for things to happen to you. Make them happen." She pauses, her lips still trembling, mouth open, her yellowed teeth glistening in the lamplight. "But don't steal any more old ladies."

"You haven't told me what you did, Lucy," I say.

"I didn't do any of those things," she says, eyes closed, her breath sucking in after every word. "Someone else did. Some young woman named Lucy Boomer, not this old thing. She ran naked, Jack. I know you don't believe it, but she did." She struggles to get her hands free of the blanket, but she can't and she becomes still again.

"I believe it, Lucy." She gives no sign of hearing. I peel back the blanket and watch her chest to see if she's breathing. I place one hand on her chest, feel the ribs, then lean to put my ear against her, hear the barely perceptible heartbeat. Then I feel her tiny clawlike hand on mine, pressing my fingers against her flattened breast.

We stay that way for several minutes until the pressure of her fingers relaxes.

Sitting up, I cover Lucy again, return to the other bed, lie on my back listening to the silence in the room, waiting for Ahna to return.

It's important that Ahna does return. She's become a part of this, of Lucy, and of me. She's no longer the girl who came along for the ride to take care of Lucy, and the journey is no longer a quest for the diaries for a long-forgotten article in a journal read by academics.

Something is about to happen. I can feel it.

CHAPTER 30

It's dim gray light when I awake. Ahna is asleep with Lucy. When she came in, or where she went in this tiny town, is beyond me. There's an occasional truck or tractor on the road and the sound of someone packing a car, footsteps in the gravel below, doors opening and closing, low voices. I dress and go downstairs past the empty front desk. I stand in the dull morning, clouds scudding overhead, watching a man and woman finish tucking suitcases into the trunk of their new Buick, hang the clothes bags in the backseat.

Carroll is beginning to come to life, a few people on the street, a coffee shop open. There's a high brick courthouse that fronts on a grassy square where a statue of a Civil War soldier stands at ease, his gun at his side. The statue is small, a slightly smaller-than-life-size man on a simple concrete pad. Nothing fancy about Carroll. I get donuts and coffee in paper cups and take them back to the hotel.

It's nine o'clock before Ahna wakes. I don't ask her where she was last night. She sips cold coffee.

"I'm going to try to find out if Lucy's family lived around here," I tell her.

"How you going to do that?"

"There's a courthouse here. That means records. I'm good at that sort of thing, researching people, finding stuff out about the past. It's what I used to do for a living."

"What if you find they were here? Then what?" She takes a bite of donut, picks the crumbs off the blanket that's wrapped around her shoulders.

"Then I'll do what I planned to do all along—I'll take her out there, show it to her, and drive like hell back to Los Angeles and put her back in the nursing home."

"You told me in Tonopah she was going to stay with relatives."

"I lied."

"And you lied about taking me to Chicago, didn't you?"

"Yes."

She pulls the blanket tighter around her shoulders, clutching it from inside with one fist, her other hand picking at the donut that lies on the battered nightstand.

"I sure as hell am not going to L.A. with you, Jack."

"Will you stay and watch her until I get back?"

She nods.

The courthouse echoes hollowly and smells of wax and disinfectant. The clerk in the records department is in the basement, a cool cavern with high metal shelves loaded with green-backed books full of property filings, court records, births and deaths, you name it. No birth certificate, no farms listed under Boomer, nothing. I tell her they may have been listed under a Czech name, but that's no help either. She tells me there's lots of Czech names in Carroll.

"She mentioned a Prairie Moon Ballroom," I tell her. "My grandmother used to talk about her father running some sort of a dance school." The lie comes easily. I've come to think of Lucy as a relative, someone close to me. Of course I don't tell the clerk I've got Lucy stashed in a hotel down the street.

Out comes another book, then another.

"Nope, never was a business under that name. But these don't go back beyond 1910. They just didn't have business licenses in those days, don't you know?" She ends almost every sentence with this same "doncha know?" She waits, expectantly.

"Of course," she continues, "there is a Prairie Moon Road. East of town." She points to a map of the township on the wall behind her. There are several little black squares along the road, bunches of them closer to town.

"What are those?"

"Farms. Farmhouses." She counts out loud, "One, two, three, four. None of them is a Boomer. I know that for a fact." A pause. "Doncha know?"

It's worth a try. I drive out the east side of town until I intersect the road. Overhead an arrow of geese crosses, their wings pumping. It's the kind of day where windows in houses are black and empty-looking, as if all were abandoned. I wish I had a heavy coat.

The first farmhouse obviously isn't it. It's a low modern ranch-style house with plastic siding and metal outbuildings. The second one doesn't look any more promising, and then the pavement ends and the road turns to gravel.

It's another four or five miles before the third one. The front porch faces the road, the house shaded by sycamore trees. The leaves turn in the wind, showing their silvery-green undersides. Already some leaves have fallen to the brown lawn underneath. The house is solid, heavy, like the heavy old men who gather by pickups on the brick streets of the small towns, their thick legs and thick chests and thick red arms encased in heavy denim. Gray and blocklike, martins' nests clogging the eaves, the house sits like a weight on the landscape, holding the farm against the prairie wind. I can imagine a quiet parlor where a child played the piano, where a nearly blind grandmother sat and knitted and waited for the grandchildren to get out the Lincoln Logs.

Old lawn furniture is piled on the front porch, and there are torn curtains at the black windows. The house looks empty, apparently not lived in.

Beyond the tree-shaded old house is the sloping farmyard, two huge old barns at the lower end, a stone ramp leading up to the open door of one, and on the far side a new farmhouse, one story, a satellite dish in the front yard. A man leans over a fence next to the stone ramp, swiveling his head to watch as I pull into the farmyard.

He comes toward me as I step out of the car.

"Excuse me, I'm looking for a farm that used to be owned by a family named Boomer."

He eyes the license plate. "California," he says, as if he were saying "Istanbul," or "Arabian Nights." At least I'm not carrying a surfboard. "You're a long way from home," he says. Behind him, over the fence, pigs snort and squeal. "What did you say their name was?"

"Boomer. It would have been a long time ago. And the original name might have been Czechoslovakian." I realize I'm sounding vague and stupid.

He squints at the pigs who grunt and swill at a wooden trough, squeaking and farting. One of them lifts a wet snout, looks at us with tiny, almost crossed eyes, then dives back into the melee.

"You say they used to live here?"

"I'm not sure. Somewhere around here."

"I've lived here for forty-five years," he says. "Before that was the Harringtons. Never heard of any Boomers."

There's an awkward pause. Behind me there's a creak of iron, the blades of an old windmill bending in the steadily increasing wind. Below it squats an iron watering trough, ten feet long, a yard wide, with a curled edge and a wire fence along the back of it. The metal legs of the windmill straddle one end. A pipe steadily drips into the windmill end. The trough is rust-brown, slick with moss where it's wet, dark, the water clear but with moss floating at the back edges. Water trickles over the lip of the trough at the far end, soaking into a muddy patch of weeds that trails off.

I look from the trough to the heavyset man in his blue windbreaker. His face is round and smooth, a graying stubble on his cheeks.

"Looks like this farm has been around for quite a while," I say.

"Old house is probably a hundred years old," he says. " 'Course the plumbing don't work and my wife says it's too dark inside. I don't guess anybody's lived in it since my father was a boy."

One more stab in the dark. "Was there ever a Prairie Moon Ballroom around here?"

He looks puzzled. Shakes his head. Then smiles. "Christ, that was in my granddad's time. Old machine shed down on the county road." He gestures farther along the gravel road that curves over the far fields.

"Used to be a place where they held dances. I don't know about the Prairie Moon name, but they called it a ballroom all right. Christ, I haven't heard that name in years. You come all the way from California to look at that?" He looks at me in disbelief.

"No, I'm just looking for some family relatives. My grandmother said there used to be a dance place on the farm where she lived when she was a girl." I can feel my pulse jumping at the discovery.

"What's your grandmother's name?"

"Lucy Boomer."

"Doesn't ring a bell."

"You mind if I go and look at the ballroom?" I ask.

"Not a bit. Although you'll be disappointed. Nothing but an old shed with old farm machinery in there." He rubs his hands briskly together. "Fall's coming," he says. "You want a cup of coffee?"

"No thanks. And thanks for your time."

"Any time," he says. He stands in the center of the farmyard and watches me turn the car around. On the road again I look back and he's still standing there.

Over the rise the fields slope toward a stand of trees about a mile off. There, in the corner of the field, is the shed, a rusting tin roof sagging in the center, weeds grown tall along the walls. I climb over the fence and push my way through the weeds, crackling grasshoppers scattering with every step like brown popcorn.

Inside it's filled with broken farm machinery and the dry musty smell of old grain and rats. The floor is wooden and, along the wall where it hasn't been scarred by years of rough use, the wood beneath the brown dust has a sheen to it as if it were a polished floor at some time. It's not a large building, maybe sixty feet long and thirty feet wide. It is the Prairie Moon Ballroom. I can feel it.

There is a thin musical whistling and it seems to fill the long room, faint, like the echo of a flute that stopped playing in a huge room and the after-echo continues, rippling from wall to wall like the diminishing rings on the surface of a still pond. But it's the wind against a window, whistling where a sliver of glass is missing. Somewhere in the distance a horse whinnies.

I squint my eyes, try to shut out the broken machinery, try to imagine this place the way Lucy described it. I try to imagine Lucy as a girl. Imagine music. The father somewhere. The brother, Robert. See the brother dance with Lucy, feel the boards of the Prairie Moon Ballroom floor move to the rhythm of the dancers. In the corner a child cranks a gramophone and the music rings from the gramophone trumpet. Lucy and Robert move easily, his hand in the small of her back, her child-woman's body following his, dancing on her toes, her body gliding the way Ahna's body glides. I want to dance with Lucy as a girl, feel her soft skin against mine. I want to be Robert, who has his back to me now, her hand caressing the back of his neck.

There is a bang at the window that startles me, but nothing is there, and then, outside, struggling against the ground, is a bird that has apparently flown against the glass. It beats its wings against the ground, rests, and with another beat of its wings is gone.

The dancers and the music are gone, too. It is a long room with broken machinery and the smell of desiccated things. I need to get back to the hotel, tell Lucy and Ahna what I have found. Suddenly there is an urgency to the day, as if I have very little time left.

Behind the shed is a field and beyond that the thin stand of trees. I walk across, my ankles turning in the roughly plowed earth. Pieces of corn stubble half plowed under stab at me. The field slopes, ending abruptly at the tree line. Below, in the flat bottom, a little creek no more than a trickle undercuts the clay bank, dribbles over half-exposed stones toward a culvert where it disappears under the road.

The farm buildings can't be seen over the rise behind me, but I don't stay. Two horses loose in the field come toward me. Horses make me nervous. The nearest one stops twenty feet off, head cocked to one side, big unblinking eyeball staring at me like a huge watery marble. It shifts its weight and the muscles on the shoulder shudder.

I move back up the field, careful to stay as close

to the fence as I can, looking sideways to keep the horses in view. I'm near the top of the field almost at the car when both horses come toward me, hooves thumping the plowed earth, and I break into a run, thrashing through the weeds next to the fence, lurching over it, tearing a pants leg in the process.

They stop short of the fence, stand there as if satisfied to have driven me off.

"I just wanted to look!" I shout. The horses stand dumbly, muscles twitching. For a moment I can imagine Lucy on horses like these. Then one of them turns and trots purposefully down the slope toward the trees.

CHAPTER 31

When I open the door to the room, Ahna is waiting for me.

"Something's wrong, Jack!" she says.

My first thought is that somebody has found us, tracked us down to this hotel in Iowa, and cops will come bursting in after me.

"What?"

"It's Lucy. She's running a fever, she's hot and she talks nonsense. I can't understand a thing she's saying." Ahna moves across to the bed where Lucy lies, looking for all the world like she's sleeping in the nursing home in L.A. Her mouth is open, eyes open, but her breath comes in short rasps and her face shines with sweat.

I bend over her.

"Lucy, can you hear me?" There is no answer. Ahna sponges Lucy's forehead with a washcloth.

"We've got to find a doctor, Jack. She's really

sick." Ahna grips my wrist and repeats herself, as if she thinks I haven't heard her.

"Lucy," I try again. "It's Jack. I found the Prairie Moon Ballroom." I take her hand, press it against my lips and say it again. "I found the ballroom. It's still there."

Her fingers move against my lips. One touches my tongue. Her raspy breath evens out.

"I knew you would," she whispers. "This morning I could feel it. Is it like I told you?"

"Yes, nothing's changed. The floor shines and there's a big old gramophone in the corner and it smells of wax and perfume and food, and I could just imagine it filled with people, just like you told me."

Her fingers stroke my jaw, rub against the stubble of my cheek.

"You're not as good a liar as you think you are, Robert," she says.

"I swear it to you. The ballroom is there, right on the edge of the road, just like you said."

"I believe that," she whispers. "But nothing stays the same. It all gets old."

"It's all there like you said, Lucy," I say, but my voice catches and I know I am crying.

Her voice, thin and far away, comes up at me again. "Take Ahna the real . . ." she says. At least this is what it sounds like.

"The real what, Lucy?"

"Take Ahna the real . . ." she repeats.

"What's she saying?" Ahna asks.

"I can't make it out. She wants me to take something real to you. The real something." I cup Lucy's face with both hands, speak directly into her eyes.

"Don't die on me yet, Lucy."

I can hear Ahna take a breath next to me. We both know what's happening.

Lucy makes one last effort. "Do something, Robert. Don't stay in one place. Do something right now." She stops trying to talk and her fingers press against my cheek for a few moments longer and then they relax, go limp. Her breath pauses, hiccups, and it, too, is gone.

Ahna says, "Oh Christ," only it's more a plea than a statement.

I feel as if a great weight has been lifted, and at the same time I feel terrified.

The window rattles sharply. The wind is up, and outside it has become gray, the sky darker.

"You've got to call someone," Ahna says. "Did you find any relatives?"

"She doesn't have any," I reply. "Everybody who ever knew her family is gone. The only thing left is a shed that used to be the ballroom."

"You already knew she didn't have anybody, didn't you?" she says accusingly. "This whole thing has been one big fucking lie after another!" She looks at Lucy's motionless body, reaches out and closes the eyelids gently. Her voice is suddenly soft, small, like Lucy's. "What do we do now?"

"Come on," I say, grabbing her wrist. I know that I have to get out of that room, that I cannot think while Lucy lies there, and I do not want Ahna out of my sight, not for one second.

"Where?" She pulls at me.

"Lucy said to do something," I say. "I don't know what she meant, but she meant something. It wasn't nonsense." My whole body feels like it's on fire, like millions of pins sticking the inside of my skin. "Come on," and I pull Ahna to the door.

Outside, the hallway is dark and someone is coming up the stairs from the lobby. I turn and we hurry down the hallway, open the door at the end and climb narrow wooden stairs. At the top there is a door. It sticks when I push against it and then, suddenly, it bursts open and we are on the flat roof of the hotel, a worn duckboard walkway in front of us, a low parapet surrounding the roof.

I can see the approaching line of clouds, and the air is yellow, like it was that evening in Tonopah when I first met Ahna. But this line of clouds has a curtain of rain in front of it, gray lines sheeting down, and in the piled darkness above, lightning flashes. The clouds are lit for an instant, then are dull again. The soft rumble of thunder comes to us.

The wind has picked up and leaves scud across the

roof, catching in the low parapet, whirling up, disappearing over the edge. Ahna looks at the approaching storm and turns back toward the door.

"This is crazy," she says. "What are we doing up here?"

"Wait." I catch her around the waist. "Wait for it."

"We're the highest thing around here. You want to get hit by lightning? What the hell are you doing, anyway?"

"Lucy said to do something. I can't think of anything else to do."

"You're crazy," she says, but she stops trying to pull away.

I let go of her, grab the bottom of my shirt and strip it off over my head, reach down and yank off one shoe, then the other. Ahna reaches down, picks up the shirt and hugs it to her chest.

"What the hell are you doing?"

I begin to strip off the rest of my clothes. The storm is closer now, the thunder more than a rumble. I can feel the dull thudding in my body. The sky around us flashes, this time brighter. I'm naked now, in the middle of Iowa, stripped of everything, waiting for something to happen. The air is charged with ozone, and it feels as if my body is charged, too. As if I could touch light bulbs and they would glow.

Ahna stares at me and then, calmly, as if it were the most natural thing to do, steps out of her skirt, strips off the rest of her clothing and turns to face the oncoming rain. I come up behind her, put my arms around her and cup her breasts. She is trembling, not just from the cold, I know, but from watching death and not knowing what lies ahead, and as I touch her skin, she shudders. I can feel her muscles tense, as if she is drawing in, sucking inward for warmth, her body taut as a drawn string, everything pulled toward the core of her body. I hold her hard against me.

The rain is on us, cold, stinging, and lightning flashes again with the slam of thunder simultaneous as it touches down somewhere close. Our skin is blue in the quick light.

Ahna turns to me, hooks her arms around my neck and pulls herself up, wrapping her legs around my waist. I realize that I'm hard, and I enter her and the rain comes down around us, turns briefly to hail and slacks off. I am weak and we sink to the duckboards, both of us shivering and laughing and crying. The rain dies to a steady drizzle and we struggle into our wet clothes, slip down the wooden stairs and back to the room.

The room is close, and smells. I open the window. Ahna strips the cover from the other bed, wraps it around herself.

"What are you going to do?" she asks.

It is the first thing either of us has said since the rain began. Outside there is the steady rattle of a drain-pipe.

"She was a neat old lady, Jack. I don't know what the hell this is all about and I don't want to know." She clutches the blanket to her chest. "Just before you came back she said to tell you the diaries are in her bank in Venice. Is she Italian?"

"She meant Venice in California."

"She said they're in your real name. Who the hell are you?"

"Jack Rabbit." The goddamn diaries.

"Like hell it is. How come she says to use your real name? And what are these diaries?" She fishes in her purse and holds up a small brass key. Obviously a safe deposit box key. "Here," she says. "Robert? Jack?" She tosses the key at me.

"I can explain," I say, and in a rush spill as much as I can. All about Schofield and the article I was writing and the rest home.

"I brought her here because she asked me to. I'm a history teacher. She has these diaries she kept while she worked in Washington, and she said she'd give them to me. She asked me to bring her to Iowa, and I thought it would be easy. By the time I got to Tonopah I was beginning to get desperate for help, and you were there. She wanted to die in Iowa, and now, goddammit, she's gone and done that. I never planned any of this. I found the farm she was born on today. I damn near got trampled by some horses, and I don't know what the hell to do with her now, but I sure as hell am not going to just walk out of here. Do you hear me?"

She stands there, still clutching the blanket to herself.

"You just put her in your car and drove off? Do they know you brought her here?"

"No, we just left. It was her idea." It sounds so incredibly lame when I say the words that a kind of hiccuping laugh comes out of me.

"Jesus," she murmurs. "This is nuts."

She turns toward Lucy, then back toward me. She drops the blanket and raises her wet blouse.

"The scar's not there," she says.

"Maybe it wasn't there all along."

"I'm not sure anymore." Her voice is tired. "I must have looked at it a hundred times." She absently runs her fingers across her skin.

"No," I say, and the words that come out are Lucy's words; my voice but Lucy's words. "That was somebody else. Not you."

"No weirdness, Jack. That's what you promised me from the very beginning. Only it's gotten very weird." She jabs her finger at me and her voice begins to break. "It's scary, Jack. I don't know what's real and what isn't."

"People imagine things all the time," I reassure

her. "Haven't you ever been really sure about something, only it turned out not to be true?"

She sits on the bed next to Lucy and reaches out to hold Lucy's hand.

I try again. "Remember me picking you up in Tonopah?"

She nods her head.

"How many guys at the counter?"

"Who the hell cares, Jack?"

"Was it five? Six? Was there anybody at all at the counter?"

"Jesus, Jack, have we all gone crazy?" She absently massages Lucy's hand in hers, as if she's reassuring Lucy that everything is going to be all right. She stares at me.

"If I say I remember six guys at the counter, does that make it six? What if you remember there were ten?"

"Jack, I'm not playing any more games." She releases Lucy's hand and stands.

"All I'm trying to say is that just because we remember something doesn't make it true. Can you see that?"

"I could feel it," she says.

"You thought you could feel it."

I want to reach out and touch her skin, put my tongue against her, feel the rhythm of her body in my ear.

"Christ!" she says to the ceiling. "I'm in a dump of a room with a dead old lady and a loony and I made it in the middle of a thunderstorm on a hotel roof." Her voice trails off.

"I'll take care of her," I say. "She wanted to die where she started."

"Well, she sure as hell didn't start here," Ahna says, sweeping her hand at the room. "Not unless she was a cockroach in some other life."

"I'm going to take her out to the farm."

"That's going to be a real surprise for the farmer. I'll bet he'll be overjoyed." She's straightening the covers around Lucy, tucking her in as if she's still alive.

"It's not like I've got a lot of choices. I mean, I can't exactly walk into a funeral home and say, 'Here's this old lady, she just died on my hands in a hotel room, I'm not related to her, and I drove her to Iowa so she could die.' They'll call the cops, and there's no way anybody is going to believe me."

"Oh shit," she says, and begins to cry. "I didn't want any of this. I don't need it." Her voice gets stronger. "This is not *my* problem, Jack." She wipes her eyes with the back of her hand.

"Besides," I continue, "she shouldn't end up in some cemetery plot where she doesn't belong. I know where she should be buried."

"Christ, Jack, leave me out of it, will you?" she

pleads. "I don't want to know." In a small voice she adds, "I just wanted to get to Chicago."

I cross to the bed, pull her up and hold her against me. The room is close and I smell the odor of death. All of Lucy's muscles have let go and she needs to be cleaned up. I need a drink. Lucy needs to be buried, and I need Ahna more than she understands.

Do something, Lucy said.

CHAPTER 32

I'm not really drunk. I've got this buzzing in the middle of my forehead and I know that I'm slurring my words, but everything else seems clear. I've been out to buy beer and gin and candles and strong soap and a white sheet to replace the one on Lucy's bed. And I've got these candles lit all around the room and the curtains shut tight. The room smells of ammonia from the soap and candle smoke, and in a while I'm going to be really drunk.

I've got Lucy's packet of pictures spread in front of me, evenly spaced in a line along the edge of the bed.

Ahna finishes washing Lucy's body, takes off the silk blouse and puts it on Lucy. She continues to work on Lucy, bare to the waist as if I'm not there, like the nurse in the rest home who undressed Lucy in front of me like she was some kind of doll, ignoring the fact that a man was standing there, a man she didn't even know. And now Ahna stands here as if I'm not sitting on the bed opposite her, as if the candles weren't lit, bending over Lucy's body, pulling on clean underwear still wet from the washing, dressing Lucy as if she were still alive, talking to her.

"Now lift your hips," she says as she slides the damp skirt on. She straightens the skirt, snaps it around the waist. She tries putting the ivory comb in Lucy's hair, but there isn't enough of it and the comb keeps falling out. Finally she sticks the comb in her own hair and straightens up.

She stands there looking at Lucy, the skin of her chest shining in the candlelight.

"I can't believe this happened to me," she says. She looks down and says again, "I can't believe this happened."

"It doesn't matter what happened," I say, trying to straighten my thoughts. I'm focusing all my attention on a spot just below her chin where the light seems the strongest, where the flickering of the candles shines against her skin in the V of her breastbone. She unconsciously fingers the spot, then looks around the room at the candles.

"Goddamn loon," she mutters. "I want all these candles out, Jack," she says emphatically. "This is bad enough without you turning it into some pagan ritual."

I think I've found what I was trying to say to her earlier, and I hold the thought but it keeps sliding off.

"It doesn't matter what happened," I say again, trying to nail the thought to the spot at the tip of her fingers. "All that matters is what's happening right now. This very minute. The past is all invention. It's an illusion that we were ever children. That these people ever existed." I touch the photograph of Lucy and her brother in their minstrel costumes, then the photo of Lucy standing on the beach. "Did you know there are people in this world who are afraid to let you photograph them?" I ask.

Ahna steps out of her skirt, crosses the room and pulls me upright by the hands. She puts her arms around me, holds me for a few seconds. "Shut up, Jack," she hisses. "I don't want to hear any more." Through the open bathroom door I can see the mirror and the reflection of the two of us pressed against each other. She releases me and gathers the photographs, places them on the nightstand and slips under the covers, moving to the far side of the bed. "No weirdness, Jack," she says, turning on her side, her back to me.

It's hard to remember. Moments after holding her body to mine, seeing the two of us pressed against each other in the mirror over the cracked sink, I have a hard time recalling her. I watch myself in the mirror for a moment, then shudder, an involuntary jerk that shivers my whole body. My grandmother would have said someone walked over my grave.

CHAPTER 33

I wake from a dream filled with birds. Long feathered herons walk on their toes, lifting their bodies the way Ahna does when she walks. Their feathers are silk gowns which they open with their beaks, cocking their heads to one side, preening for me, running feather-fingered tips of their wings down their thighs, opening their orange beaks and closing their eyes. Lucy appears in the midst of them. She's larger, and I realize that the Lucy I know has grown tinier with old age. She's dressed in a green skirt and a nubby green sweater and she wears glasses, large old-fashioned oval-framed glasses. Her skin is smooth and her long hair is wrapped stylishly on her head. She stands among the herons and beckons to someone I cannot see.

Ahna is still asleep, one arm thrown carelessly across my chest, on her back, breathing regularly through her slightly open mouth. Next to me, on the bedside stand, is the little stack of Lucy's photographs.

I pick them up, one at a time, careful not to move and disturb Ahna. I consciously don't look at the other bed, where I know Lucy lies.

The first photograph has Lucy and another young woman posing on the running board of an open car, with two young men standing on either side of them. The women hold onto the windshield posts and lean out, one foot poised above the ground, the other hand holding onto the brim of the wide hats they wear. They appear to have been stopped suddenly, the motion of the afternoon paralyzed by the camera. On the back of the photo is the date: July 1906.

I cannot reconcile the motionless girl in the photograph with the motionless figure that lies on the bed only a few feet away.

Ahna stirs in her sleep. She seems different from the girl I saw in the booth in Tonopah. Perhaps it's because I've watched her care for Lucy. More likely it's because she was a stranger then, but I know her now, have slept with her, been inside her, smelled her hair. At least I think I know her. I'm still afraid she'll disappear and all I'll have left will be these photographs of Lucy.

When I tip them against the light, the silver shines, making the dark parts rise from the surface. Ahna would look good in the hat that Lucy wears in the photograph. There is a shadow in the foreground, cast by the photographer. It's strange to think that he was there and then he moved, but his shadow remains in the photograph, along with the Lucy I never saw, young and vibrant. That Lucy no longer exists. The person I was the day I first met Lucy in Tarzana no longer exists. Ahna has changed.

Lucy no longer lies on the bed opposite. The thing that lies there was once Lucy. And that doesn't matter anymore.

Ahna stirs again and I take the opportunity to slip out of bed. When I open the curtain a crack, it's beginning to get light out. There is a bluish-gray in the street below, and ground fog mutes the streetlights. My head feels like it's in a clamp, as if my brain has dehydrated and the skull is collapsing around the empty space. Ahna sleeps. I must dress and take Lucy to the farm. That is what I must do.

CHAPTER 34

The creek is little more than a trickle. I put Lucy down on the edge; clumps of thick grass, patches of rocky dirt. From over the rise comes the whickering of a horse. There is no answer. Then I am conscious of the soft noise of water over stones. Just upstream the creek narrows and spills over a rocky ledge into a pool not much bigger than a bathtub. The volume of water is no more than a hose running in a garden; the low outcropping of rock barely protrudes above the cow-trampled ground. Moss clogs the edges of the creek, and there is the smell of decay and cow shit. Close to the ledge will be a spot that will not be plowed and, even though the creek should rise and flood, will not erode. Leaving Lucy's sheet-wrapped body by the creekside, I begin to dig next to the ledge. I sweat and it's hard work, the hole more rocks than dirt.

In the nearby cottonwoods above me crows gather to shriek at each other or me, I can't tell which.

The rock is soft, breaks up when I hit it with the shovel, and I hope the occasional clink of steel on rock doesn't carry across the fields. I want to make this hole deep enough so that no matter what happens, Lucy's body won't surface. There is a frenzy to my digging.

When I pause for breath, my chest hurts. The crows are silent, and somewhere a bird calls. It isn't like most bird calls. This one comes in single notes, as if someone were striking a piano in an empty house and the notes, hard and bright, travel from room to room, echoing from wall to wall, coming back on each other, each new note brightly shimmering.

The rocky soil turns to blue clay, clinging to the shovel in gobs, and in another half an hour I'm chest deep in the hole. I place Lucy's body in the bottom, remind myself it's not Lucy anymore, actually say the words aloud, and the crows are back.

It only takes a few minutes to fill the hole in, stamping on the dirt from time to time to pack it down, and when I'm finished, there's almost no mound. I drag some branches back and forth, scoop some gravel from beside the creek and throw it across the bare dirt, kick dried cow turds over it and stand back. It's noticeable, but cows will walk across it and trample it and after a while no one will know. I wonder if I've done the right thing. Even though it's getting gray, with the clouds coming in and the sky darkening, the fields begin to glow. The corn stubble has been disked under and a thin layer of something white, maybe chalk, catches the last light luminously.

It's colder now, a wind coming up. I shudder involuntarily, my sweat-soaked shirt evaporating. I feel flushed and hot. It's more like a cold hand that passes over my skin, the touch of the fingers of someone who has been outside on a cold night climbing into bed beside me and touching my warm skin.

I climb over the bank and start across the field. Clods of dirt turn under my shoes and my ankles hurt. I stumble back across the field until I reach the car, turn the engine on. By now there's rain slanting down. I can see it coming toward me and then little pinpricks of rain against the windshield. I turn the car heater on full blast. I'm still shaking and shivering.

The rain drifts and floats in the headlight cones like thousands of tiny moths that are suddenly sucked toward me. The radio keeps cutting in and out. Alternately it's a bible thumper yelling about salvation, and then he's drowned out by a rock and roll station. Long Tall Sally throws her shoes off and Jesus saves and when I get to the edge of town, Sally's on top.

By the time I reach the hotel the rain has become thick, slushy, as if it's about to snow. The hotel clerk, a yellowish-faced guy with a shiny pointed forehead, corners me as I cross the tiny lobby.

"Unseasonable," he says, pointing at the rain slanting down. "It's too early to snow. Something happened today," he adds, and he's looking at me accusingly. He jabs his finger at me.

"Something happened today someplace," and the last word tells me it's not me he's accusing and he doesn't know what I've been doing.

"That's why the weather is like this." He keeps nodding his head up and down as if he's agreeing with himself. "Too early," he repeats. "Somewhere out in the desert, or maybe the Russians. That's what happens. Triggers everything. Things all over the world. You'd be amazed."

I want to get away from him. I don't want him to look at me too much. It's as if I'm afraid he'll recognize me—the police will come and he'll say yeah, I saw the guy. Tall, skinny, maybe forty. He drove an old Camaro. Same day it tried to snow.

The room is empty.

There's a damp smell and there are wet towels on the floor of the bathroom. There's no point in looking for baggage—she doesn't have any and I don't know if she's gone for good. I get one of the glasses from the bathroom; they're not plastic, but real garage-sale tumblers with thick bottoms. I fill one with gin, sip it, wait. Outside the rain continues, passes, then there's the hiss of tires on the wet streets.

A noise at the door and it's Ahna. She's wet, her blouse plastered to her skin, her hair against her skull and down over her shoulders like wet black plastic.

"Jesus, where have you been?"

"Out."

"That's obvious. Christ, you're wet." I start for the bathroom to get a towel.

She sits on the bed, pulls the covers up around her shoulders. She shivers uncontrollably.

I come back with the towel, hand it to her. Holding my glass toward her, I ask, "Gin?"

She shakes her head.

"Beer?"

She nods; I crack one open.

She tips it up, lets it run in her mouth. She must drink half the can.

"What did you do with her?" she asks.

"I buried her."

"Where?"

"I buried her next to the creek."

"What creek?" Her voice is flat.

"The one she told me about a long time ago back in California. She told me about a place on the farm, and I found that place and I put her there."

She looks at me. "Christ," she says, "you just dug a goddamn hole and put her in it?"

"It wasn't that way," I say. "It was a place that meant a lot to her."

Ahna looks past me and I'm not sure if she's listening.

"I don't know," I say. "What I did seems like the

right thing. It wasn't easy. Tell me I did the right thing, Ahna."

She looks at me, tips the rest of the beer.

"I suppose it was." She shakes her head, puts the can deliberately on the nightstand next to the little pile of Lucy's photographs. "It would be nice," she says, "to be able to start all over again."

"You mean back up to Tonopah, take a ride with a trucker instead of the loon with the old lady?"

"No," she says, picking up the photos and sifting through them. "From the very beginning. Whenever that was."

CHAPTER 35

When I awake, Ahna is gone again. I'm getting used to her disappearances and lie in bed waiting for her to return, but she doesn't. I drift off to sleep again, awake to a knocking on the door and open it to find a little woman with a cleaning cart who apologizes and moves off down the corridor. It's early afternoon and there's a hazy sun out.

I dress, go out to find something to eat, come back, wait while it gets darker outside, watch the television until my eyes hurt, and still no Ahna.

I drive around town for half an hour, find all the streets, check the bars, nearly empty, the coffee shop, but she's gone.

Back at the motel I search for Lucy's photographs, but they, too, are gone. I lie on the bed smoking, waiting, suspended for the moment, not sleeping, not awake, listening.

I feel disconnected. The owl in the pool at my

apartment floating, its wings outspread on the water, seems an invention, something I made up. The scar that Ahna had and that she told me Lucy had—that, too, seems an invention. The figures in my past, my mother, my father, my brother, all seem to cast no shadow. It's as if they all happened at high noon with the light coming directly down, no shadows, no sense of movement, no more life than the packet of cracked photographs tied with ribbon in Lucy's shoe box that isn't here either. The banker's wife in Claremont, the shadowy coyotes that ran down shadowy streets, seem like parts of a movie that I watched long ago.

I know now that I need Ahna to help me make some sort of connection. She's taken the photographs with her, and I have this awful feeling that this time Ahna is gone for good, like Lucy is gone. I kill time by cleaning up the room, collecting the candles and dumping them in a paper bag, getting rid of the soiled sheet, wiping up the bathroom, folding the wet towels, even making the bed opposite, the one where Lucy died, stretching the sheet tight, smoothing it until it looks as if it had never been touched.

I go downstairs with the bag of junk, walk down the street and stuff it in a garbage can behind a bar. Back at the hotel I ask the clerk if he's seen Ahna, "You know, the young woman who came in with me? The one with the long hair?" He remembers her, but doesn't remember her going out. Maybe she went out the back way, he says, pointing vaguely at the back of the hotel.

Back in the room I lie on the unmade bed, listening intently for footsteps in the hallway, for a door opening, a car outside. Finally I fall asleep.

When I wake again it's four A.M. and still no Ahna. I count the money in my wallet—less than a hundred bucks, and the three nights here will eat most of that. Anyplace else in America they would have asked for the money up front. I feel bad about cheating Iowa, but I have no choice.

Ahna said she wanted to go to Chicago. It's maybe six hours away, and there's this slim hope in the back of my head that maybe if I go there I'll find her. It makes about as much sense as buying a lottery ticket, but I go downstairs, find the back door so I don't have to face the desk clerk, who never seems to have any relief, and find the interstate.

I spend the next two days driving around Chicago, eating minimally at fast food places, looking for Ahna. I'm overwhelmed by the dumbness of what I'm doing, knowing that there's no chance I'll find her. I have no idea where I am most of the time. A couple of times I wander into neighborhoods where obviously a middle-aged white guy should not be, and I get a flash of fear, but mostly I drive around the Loop looking at the crowds.

For most of the second day I leave the car parked

on a side street under the El and walk the lakefront, sit by the Buckingham fountain or on the steps of the art museum watching the people, looking at any woman with long hair closely, once following a woman at a half trot for a block before catching up to her and discovering she was in her fifties and didn't look anything like Ahna. I thought, for a moment, that she was going to holler for a cop.

That afternoon I gave up. The transmission began to howl again and I only had low gear, so I knew I couldn't make it back to L.A. I drove out the South Side until I found an abandoned shopping center on 159th Street that already had several stripped cars in it and left the Camaro there. I took off the license plates and sailed them onto the roof of the empty Sears store. And I took a bus to Los Angeles. I hocked my watch, and that, with the last of my cash, was enough for the ticket.

It had turned hot again, muggy, and the clouds boiled up on the horizon as we went west on I-80. We crossed into Iowa early in the evening, and it was dark when we passed the place where I had turned off to Carroll, so I missed it. I don't remember much about the rest of the trip.

Nebraska seemed endless, and then it got colder and the people in the terminals all had that hunched look animals get when they try to scrunch down inside their coats, and nobody got off the bus when it stopped unless they were going to stay off. The bus began to smell stale, and it wasn't until we got to Salt Lake City that we changed to a new bus and a new driver, who was thin-faced and intense and drove like hell, the bus rocking and rolling side to side across the desert and through Nevada. I had to change again at Sacramento to go south, and it wasn't until I woke up with the sun going down over the Tehachapis that I knew I was almost home.

I got to the apartment after midnight. Inside it smelled of stale food and stale clothes, and in the dark kitchen the refrigerator hummed loudly. I was too tired to shower. Just collapsed on the mattress and slept again until the sound of kids around the pool woke me.

CHAPTER 36

I spent the next days sitting around the pool watching the occasional stewardess sunning herself, and Eddie the manager who always managed to be out cleaning the pool when one of these creatures emerged, and the occasional mother with a child not old enough to be in school, and then my money was gone and I had to do something.

I took a bus to the community college credit union where I still had about thirty bucks in my account, and managed to talk them into a signature loan.

Being without a car in Los Angeles is like having your legs cut off, so I went to one of Cal Worthington's used car lots in Anaheim where, under the sign of smiling Cal in his cowboy hat holding his dog Spot, I got a Nissan that looked like somebody with steel-toed boots had worked over the doors. But it drove okay, and aside from a slight shudder on the freeway when it got to 45 and the latent smell of diapers and fried chicken, it meant that I'd gotten my legs back. I felt whole again.

Sitting on my desk at home was the plain brass key with the number stamped on it.

I began by calling banks in Venice.

"Hello, my name is Jack Rabbit and I've got a safe deposit box with your bank, only I think I forgot to pay the rent on it. Can you check for me?"

I'd wait until the voice came back, and when it said, "I'm sorry, Mr. Rabbit," with a tone that suggests they're tolerating some sort of junior high prank and are just waiting for the punch line, "I can't find a box under that name," I'd ask them, "Are you sure?"

Then I'd add, "I know I've got a box at Wells Fargo," or Bank of America or some other name that wasn't the one I was calling, so when they corrected me, I'd apologize for calling the wrong bank and hang up. I went through every bank in Venice, until it occurred to me that Ahna had said Lucy told her the box was "under your real name."

Maybe she meant Robert.

So I started again. At the third bank, Glendale Federal, the clerk came back on the phone and said, "Your box rent is paid through the end of the year, Mr. Boomer."

That was on a Monday.

Tuesday I got an ID at one of those storefront places on La Cienega where you swear you are who you aren't and they take your photo and you get a laminated card that won't get you served in any bar, but might get me past the teller in a bank. After all, I've got the key to the box. I used a razor blade to scratch my name off my driver's license, typed in Robert Boomer, and then folded it over several times until the mutilated license obliterated the obvious damage. Then I went to the bank.

CHAPTER 37

A clerk, disinterested in me or her job or anything else, asks what she can do.

"I need to check my safe deposit box," I say, shoving the driver's license and the ID card at her and hoping she doesn't look too closely at either one. She doesn't even bother looking, just shoves a small register back at me.

"Sign here," she says, pointing at the next empty line.

I print Robert Boomer where it tells me to print, then sign it, and realize that the B in Boomer is almost like the capital R I make when I sign my own last name. I put the brass key on the counter. She looks in a small card file, finds something, picks up the key and presses a button underneath the counter. The half door next to the counter buzzes and clicks ajar and I follow her into the open vault. She traces her finger up one row of small stainless steel doors, down another, then puts a key from her ring into a slot. She puts my key into the slot next to it, and the little door swings open. She draws out the slim metal box, hands it to me and motions toward the doorway. "There's a room you can sit in if you want to go through things," she says.

"No, I just need to take something out." She looks vacantly at the open door while I lift the lid of the box. Inside is a little packet of booklets, bound in faded morocco, a soft rose worn to a brown fuzz on the edges, held together with a rubber band. I take them out, slip them into my coat, and hand the box back to her. My heart is pounding and I'm sure she can hear it thumping off the polished metal surface. She should be yelling for security now, bringing the old guy from the front door in here with his gun drawn, but she takes the empty box, sticks it back inside the empty hole, turns the keys and holds out my key.

God, I want out of there. I have this impulse to break into a run. I can feel the surveillance cameras on me, the ones that take grainy photos of Patty Hearst and the Symbionese Liberation Army, and I can see the bald spot on my head shining briefly on television.

But nothing happens, and I drive the Nissan to the parking lot at the beach. All the benches facing the ocean are empty; the beach has that weekday hardly-used look, the sun is hard and the sky gray-blue, the kind of color that smoggy winter days produce.

The diaries read like a novel, each day a scene,

beginning with the first page written in the Chicago YWCA. I thumb through them and find, in the last one, a remembrance of a Rio trip with Hoover.

> I went out into the street. It was filled with people, all in costume, dancing, the throb of the music so loud it made my body throb. They looked at me and I knew why. I was dressed so differently. So I just took off my blouse and wrapped it around my head like a turban. It was the good silk blouse that H. had given to me, and the men all cheered when I did it. I stepped out of my skirt—it's the long gray silk one—and I tore it down the front and tied it at my neck like a cape. I had on my frilly underpants, the ones with the blue lace trim, and the men and women cheered and made a space around me. I felt like dancing and running, all at once. I took off my bra, but I have such small breasts that I guess I might pass for a boy if no one paid too much attention, and I took my lipstick and drew bright red circles around my nipples and stripes on my legs and a cupid's bow around my mouth and I danced down the streets with the dancers. The men were beautiful, all brown and glistening, and the women were beautiful, their costumes all the bright

colors of the world, and we danced and drank and sang, and the foreign words came easily to me. I didn't get back to the hotel until dawn. H. never said a word. But I could tell he didn't mind. I fell asleep in the tub, and when I awoke he was sitting on the edge watching me. I smiled and invited him to come with me. And he did.

She used initials but they were all there. She'd been a most remarkable woman, a free spirit who drifted from one to the next, Roosevelt, Taft, Wilson, Harding, a gap from 1923 to 1929 where Coolidge would have been—no explanation for it—then Hoover. I realize there is no way I can use the diaries. I'd have to attribute them to Lucy Boomer. Lucy Boomer doesn't exist anymore. She disappeared from a nursing home. How would I explain how I'd got them? All I can do is sift through them. I spend the rest of the afternoon reading. I hear her papery voice as she lies on the bed in Tarzana telling her stories. When I'm finished, I walk out onto the pier. A couple of old guys are fishing, sitting in dented aluminum chairs with a bucket of bait between them.

The Pacific is flat and shiny, the slow heave of the swells so imperceptible that it seems as if the pier itself rises and falls in a long rhythm.

And then it comes to me, as if it rises out of the

flat water, what Lucy meant when she was dying. I had
heard her say, "Take Ahna the real," and figured she
meant to take Ahna something. But here in the diaries
was what she had really said. "Take Ahna to Rio," she
had said.

I say it out loud, "Take Ahna to Rio! Christ! Go
to Rio with Ahna for the Carnival!" The old guys look
at me warily. Another nut come down to the ocean.

But I don't have Ahna, and I can't take her anywhere. I hold the soft notebooks to my face, smell the
leather and some faint smell that might have been perfume. I should go find Schofield out at the Huntington
Library, where he's probably scurrying through the
stacks looking for some obscure Hoover reference, and
beat the shit out of him. It's as if he's played some
enormous practical joke on me, got me caught up in
Lucy, and then in Ahna, and then it all disappears, goes
up in smoke, swept out to sea on a clear day, and I'm
left here on the pier with two old guys who vaguely
resemble what they're trying to catch.

There's no point to the diaries anymore. At least
not for me. I want to share them with Ahna, but I
can't. I recognize the feeling, of being caught in the
center, unable to make a decision, and I think of Lucy
saying, "Don't stay in one place," and, one at a time,
I throw the small books as far as I can into the sea.
Each one floats for a few seconds, then sinks. I watch
for a while longer. A seal breaks the water not far off,

pops its head up, then disappears. I start toward the beach. One of the old guys barks at me.

"What the hell do you think you're doing, buddy. You're not supposed to throw shit out there!"

"It wasn't shit."

"Then what the hell was it?"

"None of your goddamn business."

He looks at me for a moment, drops his gaze and says to his partner or to no one in particular, "Another goddamn weirdo."

The flat water slides gently under the pier, an oily sheen lighting the surface. Along the beach the waves slap flatly, as if they, too, are disinterested in the day.

CHAPTER 38

For the next month I make ends meet substitute teaching in the L.A. schools. Sixty-five dollars a day, with whip and chair to keep reasonable order. I don't think I teach anybody anything. I tell stories. Sometimes I tell Lucy Boomer stories, give her a new name. That keeps their attention. This is history, I say, this is the stuff you'll never read in your history books. They nod. I can tell what they're thinking. Oh God, more old-time stories from some boring old fart. But once I get into a Lucy story, they're hooked.

Mostly I'm marking time until the beginning of the spring semester, when I can get a couple of courses back at the community colleges. I've put personal ads in the *Chicago Reader*, the *Sun-Times*, and the *Tribune* on the off chance that Ahna might still be there, and I hang around the apartment afternoons and evenings, but the phone doesn't ring. By the end of the month I let the ads lapse and spend less time in the apartment.

I've cleaned it up a lot. Took out old manuscript papers, threw away old teaching files, made it look more livable, but I find I'm spending less time there.

The thing about subbing is that I can take the phone off the hook in the morning if I don't feel like working. If I work twelve days out of the month, I've got my rent and food covered, and it takes a couple more to take care of the car and gas, so I regularly take off in the middle of the week. I get out of L.A., drive up to San Bernardino to the old Arrowhead Springs or up the coast to Malibu.

Once I drove to Apple Valley, where I saw Roy Rogers or at least a good wax effigy astride a stuffed Trigger rearing up just inside the entrance to his restaurant. And next to him was a stuffed Dale Evans, or a wax figure, it was hard to figure out what was stuffed and what wasn't. The original Bullet, Roy's dog, was crouched next to Trigger's hooves, a grimace frozen on his muzzle, and it reminded me somehow of the Monrovian dog of my childhood, although not nearly so fierce.

There were a lot of tourist remarks about how gross it was to stuff the animals and put them in the lobby of a restaurant, but it occurred to me it was no more gross than Lenin's body lying in state forever in the Kremlin, or the Pharaohs.

Once I found a small stuffed dog in an antique shop in West Covina, and the shopkeeper told me that the Victorians sometimes stuffed favorite pets and used them as decoration. What a Victorian stuffed dog was doing in West Covina puzzled me, but a whole lot of old people and old things end up in Los Angeles. They're like the bits of stuff and crumbs and rubber bands that end up in the back of the silverware drawer that you never see unless you clean out the drawer, but nobody's ever going to do that to L.A.

The Victorian dog had lead shot in its belly so it could be used as a doorstop.

In November I drive all the way up the coast to Cambria Pines. I walk the beach and then when it gets dark I eat dinner in a little two-story cement-block hotel, a square building with a sign on a rusting metal pole rising from the ice plant that borders the asphalt parking lot. There is a bar downstairs and a small dining room with windows that overlook the beach.

I don't feel like driving back to L.A. so I take a room. Registration is at the end of the bar with the bartender who doesn't bother to look at my signature in the book, rings up the thirty dollars in the old cash register behind the bar.

I go through the back where it says RESTROOMS, up the narrow stairs to the room. Inside there is the faint sound of the surf booming. The only window faces the ocean. A floodlight on the beach side of the hotel illuminates part of the beach, and off in the black I can see the line of surf, the white top of the waves appearing each time it curls, coming out of the darkness as a ragged white line, then disappearing, followed by the late whump! of the waves hitting the sand.

There is a faint smell of seaweed in the room and of musty blankets. No noise from the bar below, long since empty. Only the hollow sound of the waves and the wavering, appearing and disappearing line of white in the blackness like the manes of horses floating raggedly in the wind as they move invisibly along the surf line.

I sleep fitfully, wake in the darkness with a bolt, thinking that Ahna and Lucy are in the bed next to me, only there isn't any bed next to me. It takes a moment to orient myself, explain where I am. It's the same feeling I get when I'm suddenly aware that a stranger walking next to me isn't a stranger at all, but somebody I know, as if the strange body has suddenly become inhabited by a friend who turns and says hello as if I haven't been there all along.

I lie there thinking of Ahna, remembering her bending over me, trying to remember the curve of her thighs, the roundness of her belly, until I come, lying on my back in the seaweed smell of the musty room.

In the morning the ocean is silent, the parking lot empty except for my car. Standing at the window looking out at the silent and flat ocean, I'm filled with a sensation of another room overlooking a sea. Hard blue light fills the room, the shutters are black against the sun outside. The room is warm, still. Shrill insect sounds fill the room, and I know that they are called cicadas. I know that outside the shuttered windows dusty olive trees shimmer on the hillsides. The sea has no horizon. There is a white strip on my wrist where a band has left the skin untouched by the sun. There are terraces that step down toward the village center. Voices echo from the piazza at night, sometimes music or cats fighting.

Two terraces below, an old mason builds a door frame, wood first, then bricks and stones. His helper wears a red kerchief over his hair. Sometimes the mason stops, steps back to admire his work, then looks up at me as if to ask, "What do you think?" I smile and wave at him each time. I am as old as he is, perhaps older. Yachts motor along the coast in the evening, the faint throb of engines carrying, then fading. I never tire of staring at the sea. I am waiting for someone or something.

CHAPTER 39

But there's no point in waiting here in this crummy hotel in Cambria Pines with the parking lot fading into a foggy whiteness and nothing in sight except a few sea gulls hunched on the old railroad ties that border the asphalt.

Down the narrow stairs at the door to the outside is a note taped to the wall. "Leave your keys on the hook." Apparently I'm the only one left in this place. The Nissan starts hard, belches smoke, limps down the coast until both it and the highway warm in the sun as the haze burns off.

It's mid-afternoon when I reach the apartment. Eddie is cleaning the pool and there's a package of cigarettes and a towel on one of the rusted chairs, which means there's a woman who's been sunning herself and Eddie's waiting for her to come back. He grins at me conspiratorially and says, "Not bad, not bad," which is puzzling since there's no one in sight, and it's not until

I get to the door of my apartment and find it unlocked that I realize someone is inside.

It's Ahna. Her hair is drawn up at the back of her neck, held there by Lucy's ivory ibis comb, revealing her slender neck, delicate hairs curling from it toward the bunched hair held by the comb. She wears the blouse she wore when I first saw her in Tonopah. The blouse is partially unbuttoned and Lucy's necklace of jade beads glows against her white skin. She seems radiant, rising up on her toes to move toward me. She doesn't walk, she glides.

"What the hell are you doing here?" I say. "How did you find me?"

"Somebody ran this ad for about a month in the Chicago papers looking for me. Some guy who wants to take me to Rio de Janeiro."

"Why didn't you answer it?"

"I'm not sure. I wanted to. I thought a lot about Lucy. And I tried really hard to forget about her and you. But it was as if I were reaching out to touch a flame, knowing I'd get burned, but wanting to reach out and touch it anyway. To hold my hand in it and see if it would burn."

"There's nothing to be afraid of."

"I know," she says. "I had this dream of a corn-field. I was running naked through the rows and it was hot and sticky and there was the sound of cicadas buzzing all around and the edges of the corn leaves rasped at my skin and left welts. And then I was out of the corn under the trees and there was a little creek, no more than a trickle, and you were there, sitting by my clothes. You were much younger than you are now. So I came to Los Angeles."

She says this in a voice that's matter-of-fact, as if she's come to Compton to pick up her laundry and she's stopped by to say hello. I feel like I've been clubbed by something and it's producing a blinding light behind my eyeballs, illuminating everything in the room. I half expect Eddie to come running up the stairs and the apartment fire alarm to start whanging.

Ahna draws herself to me until we are touching.

"Did you find the diaries?" she asks.

"Yes."

"What did you do with them?"

"I threw them into the ocean."

She nods, as if that were the most natural thing to have done.

"Let's go to Mexico," she says. "And drink fruit punch and tequila from flowered bowls. While there's still time."

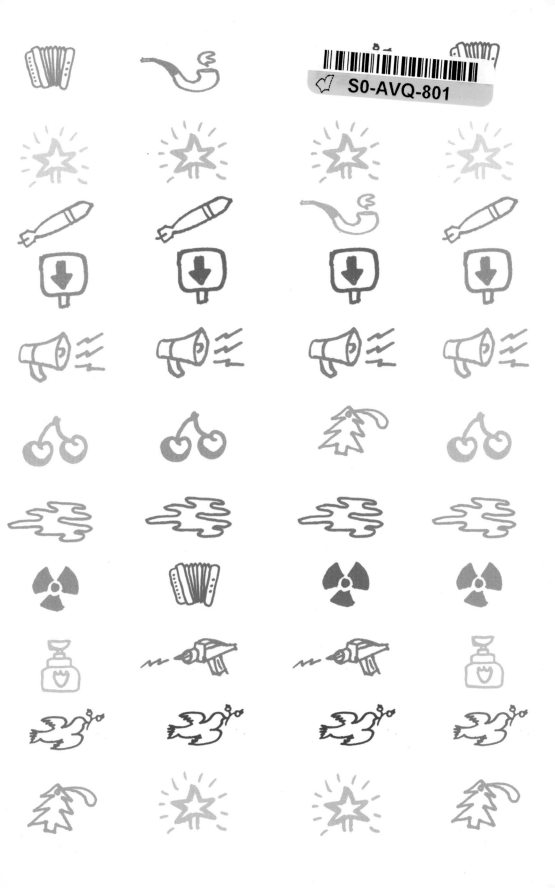

recitations by
DAVE PADDON

with illustrations by
DUNCAN MAJOR

This book is dedicated to all the volunteers at all the festivals, concerts, workshops, and venues. The quality and quantity of artistic production from our province is matched only by the the dedication and tireless efforts of all those who pitch in and give the artists an opportunity to do their stuff. Thanks to you all.

~ D. P.

For Katie, who keeps my pen light and heart full.

~ D. M.

CONTENTS

"Fog!" said Uncle Jim. "Sure, don't be talking about fog."
We were stopped, having a lunch, sitting up on a log.
We were out in the woods for a few sticks to burn,
And visibility was dropping, but 'twas no big concern.

"Where I'm from, out in Dunch Cove," he said, "the fog gets that thick
There's no good in going wooding, my son; you wouldn't get a stick.
You can cut all you want, but the trees won't come down—
They gets hung up in the fog, and can't reach the ground."

"But it's good help for the fishermen, though you'd think that it ain't;
They paint lines on the fog using fluorescent paint—
One big line from the harbour out into the sound,
Then a whole lot of small ones out to every man's ground."

"Where's Dunch Cove?" says I. "Never heard of the place."
Uncle Jim closed his eyes like he was about to say grace.
"In Placentia Bay, I s'pose, 'round Bar Haven p'raps.
It's never cleared up long enough to get marked on the maps.

"I left there one day about 40 year ago,
  When it cleared up one evening for an hour or so.
  A chopper pitched down from that funny blue sky.
  Buddy happened to spot Dunch Cove, or he would have fled by.

"Where's this to?" says he. "Dunch Cove," says I.
"Where's Dunch Cove?" says he. "Sure, you're standing in it, b'y!"
  Then he asked if I'd go with him on into town
  To prove that Dunch Cove had really been found.

"I s'pose so," says I, for it seemed a good lark,
  And I figured for sure I'd be back home by dark.
"And that's the last time I saw it," he said, draining his cup.
  Though he'd searched a few years before he gave up.

"Now come on, Uncle Jim," I said. "It can't be that thick."
  Our lunchtime was over and he was limbing out a stick.
"And that's what you knows!" he said, not missing a beat.
"In Dunch Cove, my son, it's thick enough to eat.

"Some like it toasted with molasses or jam,
  Or you can salt it in bulk for the crowd in Japan.
  Mother used to dice it with pork fat and onions,
  Or she'd mix it with mustard as a poultice for bunions.

"And it can be a hazard, if you don't watch out:
  I've seen youngsters trip on it and skin their knees out.
  And one fellow I know, who's a bit of a souse,
  Was up shingling the roof on a five-storey house;

6

"He lost track of his place, being well into the grog,
  And was five feet past the eave, nailing shingles to fog.
  Well, the next thing you know, sir, down he came, rouse-oh!
  And remember I said 'twas a five-storey house, so

"You might think he was killed, but he never got a scratch.
  He hauled out his smokes and lit up a match,
  Finished his cigarette before he hit ground.
  He would have hit hard, but the fog slowed him down."

"Go on with your lies!" I said. "'Twas never that thick!
  You're always up to some kind of old prank or a trick."
  As to our day, it was certainly getting thicker,
  And visibility was dropping now quicker and quicker.

We were down on the Burin, somewhere east of the highway,
  And would have stopped for the night if I'd have had my way.
"We could get lost in this," I called to Jim up ahead.
  But he kept right on going—"This is nothing!" he said.

Then he told me a tale I'd call taller than most,
  Of when d'Iberville the pirate was raiding the coast.
  He held all the bay from Placentia where he sat,
  But he couldn't find Dunch Cove, so he didn't hold that.

They were right for old England in the cove when they heard
  That the Frenchman was coming, and then they knew that there'd
  Be trouble that evening; things didn't look well—
  The fog was all lifted and it was clear as a bell.

Well, all hands got together to come up with a plan
To deal with the Frenchman as he drew near to hand,
For he was armed to the teeth with both cannon and ball,
And he meant to take Dunch Cove for once and for all.

When they sized up their arsenal things looked pretty poor:
Some rusty old muskets from the Thirty Years' War.
It was figured pretty generally that they didn't have a chance
And must learn how to parlez and swear oaths to France.

Then up spoke one old fellow named Azariah Dean:
"Enough of that foolishness, boys, I got a scheme
To see off the Frenchman from out of our cove.
Hark what I'm saying, if you wants to get sove."

Old Azariah had a cannon, you see,
Off one of Gilbert's ships from 1583.
He'd bought it for a bottle of rum and sixpence,
And had used it for ballast in his wharf ever since.

"That's all very well," said young Joseph Dench,
He was practicing how to say 'welcome' in French.
"A cannon alone will not do us much good.
What you going to fire out of it? Balls made of wood?"

"Something harder than that," Azariah said,
Leading the curious crowd to his shed.
There to behold in a bark pot of brine—
A way to defeat a French ship of the line.

"Hold up there, Jim," I said, stopping his tale.
   We were deep in the woods with light starting to fail.
"I'd say that we're lost and we better stop here,
   And build a bough wiffen and you'd better stay near.
   I can just barely see you there ten feet away,
   The fog is as thick as I've seen in my day."

So we built our rough shelter and made on a fire;
   It had been a long day and we were starting to tire.
   Ate a bottle of moose and a bit of hard bread,
   Rolled up a smoke and got ready for bed.

Our shelter was snug and the night was not cold,
   So Jim picked up his story right after he told
   Me we weren't really lost, though it seemed it for sure.
"This place seems familiar, like I've been here before."

So all hands was gathered, as he'd already said,
   'Round Azariah's bark pot at the back of his shed.
   And what do you s'pose that they saw lying there?
   A 12-pounder cannonball, right rounded and fair.

Azariah had figured that the Frenchman might come,
   And he'd known right away what had to be done.
   So, on a real thick day, he carved the ball out of fog,
   And put it in pickle for a proper long sog.

Well, all hands turned to and mounted the gun
On Thomas Brown's hooker, lying out in the run.
Then they hoisted all canvas and sailed out in the bight
Just as d'Iberville's big frigate hove into sight.

The hooker was shabby and a bit of a wreck,
So the French sailed near and bawled down from his deck:
'Où est Dunch Cove, in the name of Le Roi!'
His answer came point blank from the old cannon's maw.

A hole opened up on the French waterline,
And she started to settle with all hands a-flying
Over the sides into shallops and punts,
And d'Iberville savage at this worst of affronts.

It wasn't a long spell 'til the frigate went down
And the hooker became biggest ship on the sound.
In Dunch Cove that night, they had quite the spree,
With music and dancing and the grog running free.

And do you know that the ball that went through the French ship
Carried on 'cross the water with a hop and a skip,
Sank another French vessel that got in its way
Off Merasheen Island, half way 'cross the bay!"

"I don't know what's worse," I said, after a spell,
"Your navigation skills or the lies that you tell."
"Cross my heart!" he said. "Not a word of a lie!"
  Then we both fell sound to the world by and by.

Next morning the fog was as thick as before,
But Jim said, "Don't worry, boy, I knows the score."
We wondered a couple of more days in that place,
You could just see your hand stretched out from your face.

Then suddenly one day we walked into a town,
And when I caught sight of Jim, he was kissing the ground.
And then we were spotted: "Here's Jimmy back!" went the call,
Then the tears of joy flowed, oh 'twas some snot and bawl.

Well, let me see now, that was three year ago,
And Dunch Cove is not such a bad place, you know.
I married Jim's daughter last year in the fall.
Hmm... I wonder what she looks like at all?

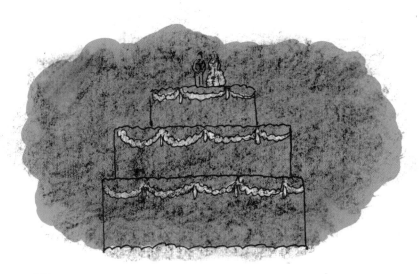

~~RABBITS~~ ~~$5/BRACE~~
DOCTORING

Now the Boiler Cove crowd was in pretty good shape—
In fact, hardly a soul had a pain or an ache;
No poxes or scurvy, angina or mumps;
No-one had piles or was swole up with lumps.

Not a one had lumbago, arthritis, or gout.
And none had bad gums or bad teeth in the mouth.
And so why such a healthy and vigourous folk?
'Twas because of their doctor, who lived up in the droke.

Now, Jim wasn't exactly a doctor, you see.
He hadn't done med school, and had only grade three.
But he could clean a moose with his eyes closed, and likewise a rabbit.
So surgery was no problem; more like a habit.

And he was good with the needle from his years making sails,
And could put arses in cats, or re-build their tails.
And there was no finer plumber, I'll say right off the bat,
So he had all the skills for doing transplants and that.

He inherited the job when old Doctor Raymond
(A proper old souse and a three-pack-a-day man)
Fell dead at the Legion one night in the fall.
They closed early that night, called off bingo and all.

A meeting was held next day in Jim's shed
To decide what to do, now Doc Raymond was dead.
But doctors were scarce, and unlikely to call
On a job in a town with no Starbucks or mall.

"No luck," said the mayor, confirming their fears.
"We'll have to make do if there's no volunteers."
So Jim stuck up his hand from where he was stood,
And said he s'posed he'd take a turn, if no one else would.

"Good enough!" said the mayor, and all hands was elated,
For all of those reasons I previously stated.
But Jim had conditions to which all did agree:
He wouldn't be doctoring while he watched *Land and Sea*.

Or when the capelin was in, or the bakeapples ripe,
And he wanted free baccy for his chew and his pipe.
And two brace a week when turr season was on—
See his boat was okay, but his motor was gone.

And so that was it, and Jim's job was lanched,
And in no time at all someone had to get panched.
Young Dickie Brown showed up to the shed,
Bowged out like a tierce and looking half dead.

Jim said he s'posed 'twas the 'pendix gone bad,
So he knocked Dickie out with some moonshine he had.
Then he opened him up with a filleting knife,
Cleaned up with Javex he scrounged from Dick's wife.

In no time at all, sure, the patient was fine,
And Jim sewed him up with monofilament line.
He said that his fee would be two cord of wood.
"All birch, Dick," he said, "'cause var is no good."

Now the next case Jim had was Uncle Bill Shea,
Who was white as a ghost when he walked in one day.
Jim sized him up and said, after a spell,
"The timing is off on your heart, Uncle Bill."

"You wants a pacemaker," was the next thing Jim said.
"Here drink some of this, and lie on the daybed."
Soon Bill was asleep and he started to snore,
While Jim looked for parts at the back of his store.

Some Marette connectors and number 12 wire,
And a 15-amp fuse, 'cause you wouldn't want higher.
Then he opened Bill's chest with a chisel and mall,
And saw right away what he had to install.

First thing that went in was points and a coil
From his old outboard motor that burned too much oil.
Then a chainsaw spark plug and a brand new condenser,
And from his wife's old K-Car, a PC valve sensor.

And to finish the job, and at Bill's wife's request,
A pull cord, in case Bill had cardiac arrest.
And so that was it, Bill's heart was re-sot
For a tub of salt herring and Bill's old barking pot.

Now, Jim wasn't so handy when it came to obstetrics,
So he called for some backup when young Collette Dicks
Showed up one Tuesday about half past two,
As big as a puncheon, two weeks overdue.

Jim's Missus Josie'd had ten kids altogether,
And she came right away when Jim went to get her.
He stood off from the daybed and said, "What you think, Jose?"
"Get some powder, Jim," she said, "and we'll quill her, I s'pose."

Jim had black powder from the muzzle-loader days;
"Better draw some," he said, "just like Jose says."
Then he found a goose feather and cut off both ends,
And had a nice little tube, sir, right straight with no bends.

Jose looked at the tube to make sure it was right,
And put powder in the wide end and packed it in tight.
"Now, Collette," she said, "this should do it, I s'pose."
And with that, she blew the works right up Collette's nose.

Next thing Collette sneezed, sir, 'twas just like the thunder,
And the legs on the daybed just about buckled under.
Then a baby came out and started to bawl,
And then another, right after, 'twas a twin after all!

16

Collette wanted Jim and Josie to name 'em,
And so a notice appeared in our paper, the *Bayman*:
"Arrived January the 8th, at about half past six,
Johnson, and his twin brother Evinrude, Dicks."

Now things were quiet for a while, which suited Jim to a tee;
He had firewood to cut down and cleave up, you see.
Then one day last fall this fellow came to town
From the government, and started to call Jim right down.

"You're no kind of doctor with no licence to practice,
Or at least that's what I'm advised that the facts is.
I insist you desist and accompany me
To the local detachment of the RCMP."

Then he turned on his heel to go back to his car
With his nose in the air, but he didn't get far.
He tripped on a crankshaft Jim had on the floor
Then down he went, rouse-oh! And he let out some roar!

What a state he was in, with his crying and choking
And screeching and bawling that his leg must be broken.
"You're a doctor," he said, "you must help! I insist!"
Jim said, "Lie on the daybed and drink some of this."

When Jim looked at the leg, he said, "My, what a mess,
Looks like it'll have to be a transplant, I guess."
So he picked out a bone from some spares in a heap,
And said, "Now that's from that black bear that killed Josie's sheep."

Well, when buddy woke up, he thought the world over Jim,
And announced that he'd no longer be hassling him.
He said, "I must have been given some bad information."
"Not bad, eh?" said Jim. "For a bare-bones operation."

Well, Jim is still at it, the only doctor in town,
And buddy from the government is still hanging around;
He spends all his winters asleep like a lump,
And in the summer he hangs 'round the Boiler Cove dump.

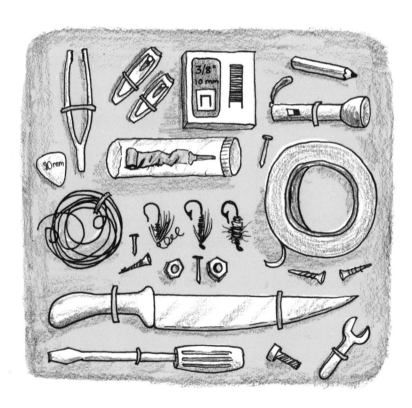

Now 'twas the middle of July month, one day last year,
Jim was out on his bridge with a bottle of beer;
He'd been hard at it all day, out cutting his grass,
And then putting in sparbles on his old iron lass.

He'd fixed up a leak in his porch with some tar,
Made an oar for his punt with a nice stick of var.
He was thinking that capelin might roll on the beach,
When Aunt Josie let out with the dirty big screech.

"My jumpins, maid!" he said, as he ran in the house,
"I s'pose now the cat never got every mouse."
"Mind now!" she said. It wasn't mice that had drove her.
'Twas the toilet blocked up and run out all over.

"Hmmph," said Uncle Jim. "I'd sooner it was mice."
He had a job to do now, and it wouldn't be nice.
He knew that he needed some help right away,
So he called up his buddy, Uncle Bill Shea.

20

But is 'buddy' the right word? Well, now, that depends.
They were the best kind of enemies, and the worst kind of friends.
There was just about nothing on which they'd agree:
If Jim wanted coffee, Bill wanted tea.

If Jim's rodney was anchored, Bill's punt was moored;
Jim was a Chev man, Bill drove a Ford.
Jim was a Leafs fan, Bill liked the Habs;
Jim's wood was in junks, Bill's was in slabs.

What Jim called a 'haul-off', Bill called a 'frape';
Jim liked the cod's heads, and Bill liked the napes.
Jim thought that Coaker'd been right all along;
Bill thought the man was as stunned as a prong.

So being best friends, when they weren't in a fight,
Jim called up Bill and told him his plight.
"Be there right away," Bill said, "I just had a scoff.
I'll get some gear, you get the ground all scrope off."

Now Bill had equipment for this kind of thing—
A '58 Dodge truck with neither shock, sir, nor spring.
In the back on its side was an old oil tank
That he'd bought for five bucks from his son-in-law Frank.

He stopped at the hole Jim had dug in the ground
To the septic tank top, about two feet down.
Jim had the cover removed from the tank,
And certainly you know now that that never stank!

"Hmmm," said Uncle Bill. "I'd say there's no doubt
  She been got over filled and wants be pumped out."
"You got something for that?" Jim was sot on a stump.
"Yes, b'y," said Bill, "help me lift down pump."

With the pump on the ground, Jim looked at it closely.
"What kind is it?" he said. Bill said, "Well, mostly
  A Honda, I suppose, but the motor was small
  And went all abroad on a job from last fall."

"I put in something stronger," Bill said, clearing his throat,
"Last year when I scrapped out my old motor boat."
"Hmm," said Jim, sitting back on his stump,
"A 4-horsepower Acadia septic tank pump!"

Bill ran a hose from the pump to the tank in the back of the truck,
And another from the pump to the tank full of muck.
Then he primed the old engine, gave the flywheel a flick,
And had her running like that; yes sir, Bill was some slick.

The tank started to empty at a pretty good rate.
Bill looked pleased with himself, and he started to prate
About the stuff he could build and how handy he was—
He probably should have stayed quiet because…

See, a 4-horsepower Acadia got a fair bit of torque,
And this one was hopping around like a cork
That you'd use for a bobber when you're out on a pond
And you got a nice trout or an eel hooked on.

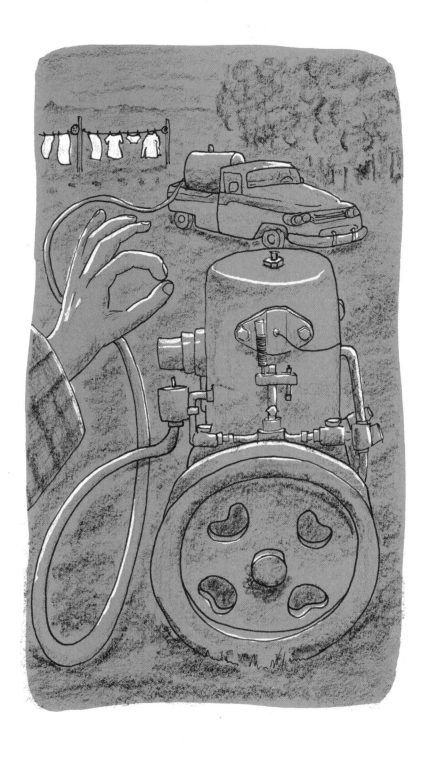

The pump, sir, was headed right straight for the tank,
And each time it hopped it would give a good yank
On the hose in the tank in the back of the truck
Which was filling up quickly with septic tank muck.

Both of our heroes saw at the same time
What the outcome would be, and they both started trying
To get at the kill switch that Bill had rigged up,
And shut down the quickly migrating put-put.

But the pump had a mind of its own or you'd swear
And would dart at the boys if either got near.
It seemed that the three were in some kind of dance
When Aunt Josie came out for a look, just by chance.

"My jumpins," she said, and she furrowed her brow.
"What in the world are those two at now?"
And here's where it gets really interesting, see—
The hose in the tank in the truck popped out free.

Now, remember what I said about Acadia torque?
And how this one was hopping around like a cork?
The hose end was snapping around like a whip
And with septic tank contents was letting her rip.

Aunt Josie had out a line of clean clothes—
They got it first from the untethered hose.
Uncle Jim's pickup was next to turn brown,
And, yes sir, you guessed it: the windows were down.

Uncle Bill got it next from his toes to his head;
He'd almost made shelter in Jim's old woodshed.
Jim had found cover behind his back fence,
And he would have stayed there, if he'd had any sense.

But he poked up his head for a quick look at Bill,
And he laughed at the sight of him covered, until
A blast from the hose got him right in the face.
He stopped laughing then, being put in his place.

The pump had now hopped 20 feet, I would say,
Wreaking havoc on all, if I can put it that way.
But it must have been tired of its fine little prank,
'Cause with a last blast at Jose it hopped into the tank.

Not long after that Bill scrapped out his pump,
After fishing it out of the tank where it sunk.
Him and Jim don't talk to each other, if able,
And Aunt Josie says the two of them are stunned as a grapel.

But Bill got new plans for the Acadia 4:
With a smaller flywheel that he found in his store,
And some minor adjustments to the old carburetor—
A 4-horsepower Acadia kitchen garburettor.

Nobody knew how long Uncle Jim
Had been flying airplanes, not even him.
They knew for sure that he'd started in the war—
But which war he'd started in, they weren't really sure.

He'd flown DC 3s in the Second World War.
On the Berlin Airlift, he'd flown a DC 4.
He'd flown DC 6s, DC 7s, and 8s,
And everything that Boeing pushed out of their gates.

He'd flown Beavers on skis and Otters on floats,
Dropped water on fires from old flying boats.
Flown in the Arctic and the tropical climes,
And circled the globe any number of times.

But there was no flight that Jim liked to do half so well
As a flight home to St. John's, and so it befell
That not long ago, on a fine winter's day,
He departed Toronto heading east for Torbay.

His co-pilot that day was a youngster named Tim,
About 12 years old with peach fuzz on chin.
He was only just hired, 'twas his very first day.
"Captain, sir," he said. "Should I do the PA?"

"I'll do it myself," Jim said, grabbing the mic.
"That's my crowd back there and I know what they like."
So he cleared his throat loudly and said right off the bat,
"Ladies and gentlemen, what are ya at?"

"We'll be passing by Ottawa, and we'll pass Montréal.
But I'm not fussy about either, so what odds at all?
Then it's off 'cross the Gulf and in over Cape Ray,
By Fox Roost, Burnt Islands, Rose Blanche, and Connoire Bay.

"By Grand Bruit and Burgeo, Francois and McCallum,
By Hermitage and Gaultois, Boxey and Belleoram,
Bay L'Argent and Dunch Cove, Haystack and Dildo,
And Hopeall and Riverhead, where the *Kyle* is, you know.

"Then over the bay and over Bauline
For a landing, I dare say, on runway 16."
Then he forgot about the mic, and said after a while,
"Now then, I'm starving, where's my bottle of swile?"

Right away there arose a great noise from the back.
"My jumpins," said Jim, "that's the crowd from Fort Mac!
Sit down and be quiet!" He let out the bawl.
"I got 19 bottles, enough for us all."

Not long after that the smell of the seal
Was all through the plane as the boys had their meal.
One welder from Chance Cove said to the young maid,
"Any chance the skipper got a bit of hard bread?"

As they dodged along nicely at 35 thousand,
Jim said, "Should check me slips today, I allows," and
Just off Port aux Basques he took her down low,
To see if he could see any turrs on the go.

He could see that the waters weren't very turry
As he waved at the skipper on the Port aux Basques ferry.
"He's a buddy of mine," he said to young Tim.
"Yes, Captain, but shouldn't *we* be higher than *him?*"

Having finished his bottle of flipper and liver,
Jim turned left and flew up the Bay du Nord River.
"But, Captain," said Tim, "won't we be late?"
"A little," said Jim, "but the crowd home will wait."

As they flew up the river at about treetop height,
Jim said, "Lots of partridge around, but not a rabbit in sight.
And look at that moose stood up there right proud—
Got to mind that one, now, for the Turnip Cove crowd."

As they dodged past Mount Peyton something powerful and sleek
Passed on the left, just the pure yellow streak.
"It's a UFO!" said Tim. "I'm sure, yes I am!"
"That's the wife's father," said Jim, "on his old 12 Elan."

28

Then a voice came on the radio, "Want to stop and boil up?"
"I got some roast capelin and saltwater duck."
"Not today, boy," said Jim. "I just had some swile,
  Think we'll go out to Fogo and watch hockey for a while."

  A few minutes later they were holding at Tilting,
  Where the game was unfolding and Tilting was wilting.
  Jim called the play for the crowd in the back:
"I know now young Paddy never give Billy some crack!"

With the score 6 to 1, Tilting had no escape.
Jim said, "Let's go to Bonavista and fly 'round the Cape.
Young Ryder's aboard, and I'd say that he'd 'ruther
Take a buzz by his house and wave to his mother."

"But, Captain," said Tim, "I'm not really sure how
  We'll get to St. John's—we're low on fuel now!"
"Don't worry," said Jim. "I won't put us in peril.
  Look there's Mrs Ryder and Mayor Fitzgerald."

"Who wants a coffee?" Jim said on the PA,
  As they flew down the north side of Trinity Bay.
  No-one seemed to mind when the first place they arrived to
  Wasn't town, but the Clarenville Tim Horton's drive-through.

"Eight dozen honey glazed!" Jim put in his order,
"And one of those nice cakes with hearts round the border.
  It's the wife's birthday cake and she likes one in yellow.
  And a puncheon of coffee, de-caf for the young fellow."

When all hands had their orders and were comfortably sot,
Jim took off again from the mall parking lot.
"Captain, my Captain," young Timothy said,
"I'm not liking the math going on in my head.

"By my calculations we won't make Torbay—
We'll run out of fuel before we're half way!"
"Yes, buddy," Jim said, "let's get Bessie a drink
At the Goobies Big Stop; I got some coupons, I think."

And so they pitched down and turned in by the moose
Filled her up with supreme for a little more boost.
Jim said, "I wants the *Downhomer* for the puzzles and that.
What's a three-letter word for 'feline'?.... Oh yeah, 'cat.'"

Airborne again, young Tim said, "At last!"
But Jim said, "No hurry now, we got thousands of gas.
We'll trim along the shoreline for a nice little randy,
And land when we wants to 'cause town's only handy."

They flew down the Cape Shore and around Cape St. Mary's,
Over Branch where Jim said, "That's some spot for berries!"
Over St. Mary's Bay and in over Cape Freels,
"Now, buddy," said Jim, "you like jigs best, or reels?"

Well, Tim had no idea what the Skipper was saying,
And if he should smile and nod or maybe start praying.
Jim said, "There's a bit of time yet, before we gets moored again."
And with that he produced a small button accordion.

"Lay hold, William Oldford, lay hold, William White!"
Jim sang it all wrong and he never played right,
Then he got all overcome and started to bawl—
"Poor Kitty," he sobbed, "how stunned was buddy, at all?"

Heaving a sigh, Jim put down his box,
And said "Now, here's where the *Florizel* went on the rocks.
We'll take a dart inshore when we gets to Renews
And check on my cabin in back of Fermeuse."

Not long after that, as they passed Witless Bay,
Jim said he s'posed that he'd land now and call it a day.
He said, "Call up the tower and get me the weather
'Til I puts on me specs so I can see better."

"Windy," said the tower, "and a little bit dunch;
I can still see my nose but I can't see my lunch.
Watch out for small cars and flying tree trunks,
And Bell Island blew away somewhere out round the Funks."

"We should divert!" said Tim, his voice starting to croak.
"Some chance now," said Jim. "I got fish in to soak."
"But I'll put the boots to her," he told the young lad,
"And get on the ground now before it gets bad."

Well, they started to roll and to bounce and to dip,
Had to go hard a starboard round an oil-rig ship.
"Now, buddy," said Jim, as he dodged round a log,
"What's a three-letter word for 'canine'?... Oh yeah, 'dog.'"

They finally touched down with a bit of a flop,
Taxied into the gate and came to a stop.
Tim wiped the sweat off his brow with a hanky.
"I got an old punt like this one," Jim said. "She's right cranky."

As the people got off, the air filled with the sound
Of CFAs bawling and kissing the ground.
Said one, "He's a hero to land in this mess."
Said a bayman, "Not bad for a townie, I guess."

Jim still flies the planes, and one day last year
He was just after eating a bottle of turr.
He told a planeload of people, "There'll be a delay—
The capelin is in down to Great Barasaway."

Vessels

Uncle Jim Buckle and Uncle Bill Shea
Were out on Jim's bridge, one fine summer's day,
When a racket broke out, as is often the case,
Over whose boat was better and who'd win in a race.

And whose could stand the most lop or hold the most fish,
And which one was cranky and which one was nish,
And which one was better for out at the turrs,
And which one rowed scow-ways and which one leaked worse.

Sure, they couldn't even agree what it was that they had,
And that's when they turned off from crousty to mad.
"It's a rodney," said Jim, "and you're stunned as a killick!"
Bill said, "'Tis a punt, boy, you foolish old twillick."

Then Jim said he'd settle things, for once and for all,
By telling the tale of what happened last fall;
He was out in his.....vessel for a meal of cod,
With his good buddy Phonse and…ah…Phonse is a dog.

Well, Jim had ten fish and was headed for the tickle,
Where he figured he'd split them and put them in pickle.
When up roared the Fisheries in the big zodiac,
And came alongside Jim with a bit of a smack.

Then this fellow started clucking like a foolish old hen,
"You're 'llowed only five fish, sir, how come you got ten?"
"Don't be so stunned, b'y," was Jim's quick response,
"I got five for me and I got five for Phonse."

Well, that didn't get Jim far, as well you might know.
"Heave to," said the Fisheries, "and we'll take you in tow."
"Some chance now!" said Jim, as he picked up his oars,
"You won't be towing me with that old tub of yours."

"Now, sir," said the Fisheries, "I think we'll call the shots.
We got two big Hondas and can do 90 knots."
"Mind now," said Jim, "if I don't burst a whit.
I'll leave you behind, and I won't break a sweat."

Well, Jim set his oars and he started to row,
With the Fisheries coming along behind pretty slow,
'Til all of a sudden things was all spray and froth,
Jim had hit 20 knots with his vessel planed off!

Well, Jim picked up speed and it wasn't long before
The Fisheries was behind by a mile or more.
Then the order came down: "Boys give her full speed
Before that old fellow makes fools out of we."

Soon they hit 90 knots and started to close
The gap Jim had opened, couple miles I suppose.
Then just as they caught up and hauled alongside,
Jim sped out of sight and left the Fisheries to bide.

"Humph," said Uncle Bill, "I'd like to know how you
  Got her up over 90, that's all I can do."
"Well, now," said Jim, "I was tired, you see,
  So Phonse took a turn. Yuh, he's faster than me."

"Well I s'pose 'tis all true," Bill said, after a spell.
"But put on the kettle now and wait 'til I tell
  You what happened to me when I was just a young tar,
  Oh, long time ago 'twas, back in the war.

"I was out at the turrs with my young fellow Mark;
  We were headed for home and it was just getting dark.
  We had a bit of a breeze but it wasn't too bad
  'Til Mark went and lit up a smoke that he had.

"Then this big German sub came up from below,
  And give us some fright, yes sir, no, I know.
  He was 'bout a gunshot off and right on our lee.
  And he hauled off and fired a torwizzin at we!

"Well, sir, Mark was some cross and I wasn't too glad,
  So I up with the old muzzle loader I had.
  And to show them we didn't think too much of their joke,
  I let drive with six fingers and shot out their scope.

36

"Down went that sub in ten seconds or so.
'Now, Mark,' I said, 'S'pose we'll let that one go.'
'Some chance, now,' he said. 'I wants a word with that captain,
So take a good breath now, Father, we're going down after 'en.'

"And that's what we did, sir, not a word of a lie!
Fifty fathom or so until, by and by,
We caught sight of that sub down there in the dark,
Then I grabbed two good lines and passed them to Mark.

"He made fast to her rudder with both of those lines and
Took two or three hitches up into the risings.
By this time, we'd been down ten minutes or near,
And 'twas time to come up for a breath of fresh air.

"So we started on up, heading west for the shore,
The sub was going east at ten knots or more.
Well, we took up the slack and that sub brought up solid,
Then they give her the gas, sir, like the cat that was scalded.

"'Twas touch and go, I s'pose, for five minutes or more,
'Til Mark come on hard with the big sculling oar.
Then the boys on the sub saw 'twas no use,
And we hauled that old thing right back home to Renews."

"Humph," said Uncle Jim, when he spoke by and by.
"Cross my heart, sir," said Bill, "not a word of a lie."
He'd used the old sub right up to last year.
"'Twas the clear thing," he said, "getting rum from St. Pierre."

"I s'pose, now," Jim said. "Oh yuh," Bill replied,
"I know now we never gave that sub crowd some ride."
   Then the two of them sat there, and no more was said,
   And if looks could have killed, sir, they'd both have been dead.

   Now I'd been sitting there listening to all this, you see;
"Enough, boys," I said, "shake hands and agree."
"And that's what I won't!" Jim said, right off the bat.
   Bill said for sure he was in favour against that!

   Then they went right back at it, about rodneys and punts;
"Give it up, boys," I said, "or I'm leaving the once!"
   Then a funny thing happened on that bridge, by and by,
   And don't forget now, I'm the one who don't lie.

"Will you two shut up?" rose a voice from below.
"I'm trying to get a nap here, in case you don't know.
   It's not a rodney, or a punt," the voice said between yawns.
"It's a dory, end of story, now be quiet," said Phonse.

Now not long ago, in the republic of d'oil,
Uncle Jim and Uncle Bill had the kettle on to boil.
"15 six," said Jim, "and two pair is ten!
I see on the news we're a 'have province' again."

"Yes, b'y," said Bill, "with McMurray not there,
Since our fellows got homesick and moved back to here,
And the price of a barrel is got right out of hand
'Tis a job to put gas in my old 12 Elan."

Jim read the paper while he waited to play,
And said, "Looks like the government must be doing okay.
They got out a tender, right here on page eight,
For a Labrador tunnel under Belle Isle Strait."

"Oh yuh?" said Bill, as he put down a card,
"I might bid on that, shouldn't be too hard.
Take a month I s'pose," he said with a shrug.
"Sure my wood is all split and my pratties all dug."

40

Well, Jim roared out laughing, "A month now!" he said,
"I could do it in a month, and spend half that in bed."
Bill didn't like that much, and he challenged out Jim;
He said he figured he'd get across faster than him.

And faster than time, sir, the boys were rowed out;
There always was something they were rowed out about:
Like whose boat was better, or who grew the best cabbage,
And a Canadians/Leafs game could turn the boys savage.

"That's it then," said Jim, giving Bill a hard look.
"I'm leaving tomorrow from Green Island Brook."
Bill said he'd go southbound from in Forteau Bay.
"I dare say," he said, "they wants a tunnel each way."

About 3 in the morning, Bill got out of bed,
And went out in back of the house to his shed,
Where he changed out the track on his old snowmobile
For one with 15-inch cleats made from reinforced steel.

Then he roared 'cross the straits to the Labrador side,
Early enough so he thought, 'til he spied
Uncle Jim in the landwash at Green Island Brook.
Jim was looking right back and 'twas some dirty look.

He was just getting ready to start on his dig,
Strapped in the seat of a queer-looking rig.
P'raps 'odd' is the right word, you never seen odder—
'Twas a make-and-break-powered ten-foot-long podauger.

Jim spun his flywheel and put his augur in gear,
Then bawled at the crowd gathered round to stay clear.
Then as he went under and clean out of sight
He took one last mark on the Point Amour Light.

Now Bill, in the meantime, was a quarter mile down
With a good lead on Jim, 'til he got all turned around.
See his sense of direction was not all the best,
And he was headed up the shore toward West St. Modeste.

The point on Jim's auger had a couple of flaws,
And he wasn't going as straight as he thought that he was.
When he thought he'd crossed over and came up for a look,
He was in Green Island Cove, right by Green Island Brook.

Bill figured for sure he was over by now,
But when he came to the surface, he found that somehow
His course had been wrong, sure mile after mile,
And he was up on the southwestern shore of Belle Isle.

"My blessed!" he said, when he saw where he was.
  He thought he been headed right fair straight across.
"Oh, well," he said, digging down again quick,
"It's a fine place to stop for a lunch or picnic."

Jim, in the meantime, was back down below,
Watching his compass and taking it slow.
But a big iron deposit meant his compass was out,
And in fact, he was headed straight east just about.

He'd sharpened his augur and was making good time;
He'd topped off his gas and all systems was fine,
So he tipped back his seat and put up his feet,
And in no time at all, sir, he fell fast asleep.

Bill was gone wrong again, now, 'twill be no surprise,
And was having a lunch with a nice bunch of b'ys.
'Cause that's who you run into now, any old time,
Your tunnel runs into a Cape Breton mine.

He sang a few songs with the coal mining b'ys,
Then he went to set course, having two or three tries.
But it wasn't so easy, as you may agree,
With neither the Pole Star nor Dipper to see.

Now Jim had been up pretty late the last night,
Watching the Habs beat the Leafs again, right?
So he never woke up for ten hours at least,
While his auger bored on heading straight to the east.

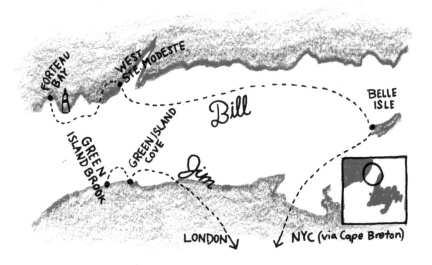

"Where'd Bill come up next?" I can now hear you say.
Well, you wouldn't believe me, so I'll put it this way—
He was having a beer with his first cousin Pat and
Her husband who lived right in downtown Manhattan.

Jim finally woke up with a bit of a fright,
He'd come out in a tunnel all lit up and bright.
People were staring, and he felt kind of silly,
Then he read out a sign on the wall "Piccadilly!?"

"Oh my," he said, "I'm a bit off my mark!
Can't be the Port au Port one with the park."
He cursed on himself for his extra long nap,
When some Englishman spoke up and said, "Mind the gap!"

Well, that was enough for both Jim and Bill;
Of the tunnelling business, they'd both had their fill.
They came to the surface and got home that night,
Feeling too foolish and too tired to fight.

But 'twill be all to the good in 2 ought 41,
When the contract is over and when we can run
A power line east to light London and fork
Off another one southward to light up New York.

BERRIES

Uncle Jim Buckle and his new woman Dot
Liked to pick berries, they liked it a lot.
The same could be said for Ross and Bill Barbour,
Two brothers who also lived in our harbour.

In fact, rivals is what you could say that they were,
And you wouldn't say friendly ones either, no sir.
All summer they'd be out on the barren and bog
Trying to out-pick each other in rain, sun, or fog.

The Hundred Years' War is what we call it 'round here,
And how it got started, nobody's clear.
Except for yours truly, I remember it yet—
Uncle Jim was at the berries with his first woman, Bette.

They were out on the barrens with two tumblers to fill
When out of the burnt woods strode Rossy and Bill.
Ross looked at their haul and said, kind of low,
"Not going all out are they, brud? No, I know!"

46

"Like to see you do better!" Uncle Jim said, incensed.
And so the challenge was issued and hostilities commenced.
The brothers got busy, and as the daylight grew dim,
Had a small salt-beef bucket full right to the brim.

The skirmish continued for the rest of the fall,
'Til the snow came and covered up berries and all.
Then a temporary ceasefire was put into place;
But both parties schemed to continue the race.

All winter Uncle Jim and his missus made plans
And went door to door scrounging old pots and pans.
By springtime, the brothers (who'd stayed out of the clubs)
Had a thousand Imperial margarine tubs.

Soon enough, the battle was joined once again,
With half-starving bears drove back into the den.
The barrens were ripped with the maulings and tearings,
And the bakeapples picked while still hard as ball bearings.

Who threw the first rock? Well, we don't really know.
Both sides blamed the other, as well you might know.
Next thing we knew, they had rifles and camo;
It was all we could do to keep stealing their ammo.

The brothers rented time on a spy satellite,
And rigged up a cannon on an old Honda quad trike.
Uncle Jim bought some land mines from a guy on the net.
(Yup. That's what became of his first woman Bette.)

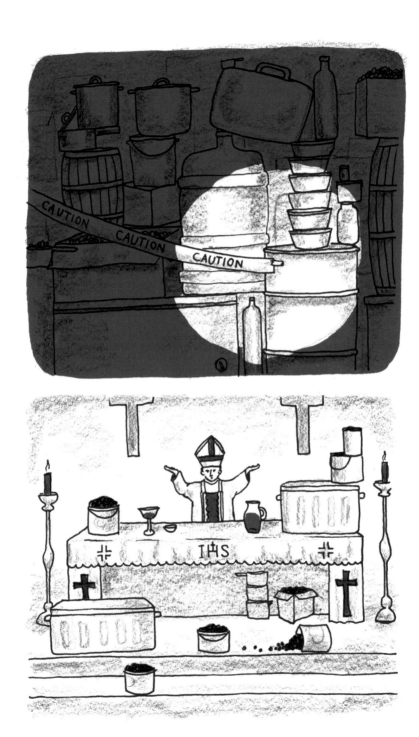

48

It wasn't too long before he married again
To a woman best described as Attila the Hen.
But now a new problem loomed on the horizon:
A shortage of space to store berries, jams, and pies in.

The brothers had ten freezers full right to the top,
And a cold-storage unit scrounged from the Co-op.
Uncle Jim bought our fish plant, closed many a year,
And stored all of his and Dot's berries in there.

'Round about this time I started to think
That what they all needed was a really good shrink.
So I put down my copy of the *Telegram* funnies,
And ordered a book called *Psychiatry for Dummies*.

"Seems pretty simple," I said, half way through.
"Guess I'll go straighten out Jim, and maybe Dot, too."
So I strolled to their house in psychiatrist style,
And said, "Listen, you two, you've been in denial."

"And that's what we haven't," Jim said, "by the damn!"
He was stirring a ten-gallon boiler of jam.
"Perhaps we might go, although I predict
That the 'Gyptians got everything over there picked!"

Having lost a little psychiatrist pride,
I concluded the Buckles would stump Sigmund Freud.
Perhaps I'll do better, I thought, 'cross the harbour,
With my other two patients, Bill and Ross Barbour.

They were out in their shed with a welding machine
At work on the hull of an old submarine
With refrigerant tanks and two diesel compressors—
Oh yes, Rossy and Bill were quite the professors!

"Now, boys," I said, "here's my diagnosis:
Obsessive behaviour and acute *pickanosis*.
I think I can help if you'll only take heed—
A good 12-step program is what you guys need."

Bill slowly emerged from a torpedo tube,
Covered in what must have been torpedo lube.
"We've been on one for years now," I then heard him say.
"Berries always look better just 12 steps away."

And so ended my budding career as a shrink,
Much longer and I think they'd have drove me to drink.
By this time they'd run out of storage again,
Having filled up our church, then our new Lion's Den.

Uncle Jim had rented an old supertanker,
And filled her to bursting as she lay to her anchor.
The brothers had small vessels of various kinds,
And had filled up Bell Island's old iron-ore mines.

Then one day the old vessel's chain gave away,
And she ended up drifting 'round Conception Bay.
Meanwhile, below in the tunnels of rock,
Ross and Bill's berries had turned all to rot.

The pressure was building from the gasses released;
The old ship was drifting from the west to the east.
Then as she passed over the undersea shafts,
The pressure released in one almighty blast.

Her hull overstressed by the undersea fart,
The old ship went down and she broke all apart.
When things finally settled from that almighty wham,
The whole of the bay wasn't nothing only jam.

Well, the four of our nitwits were summoned next day
To magistrates' court where the judge had his say.
"Community service down at Purity Foods
Making salt water Jam-Jams and other baked goods."

It seemed that the war would go on unabated,
'Til one day they discovered that they were related.
Now they're all the best kind and don't even get snappy;
The barrens are quiet and the bears are all happy.

So now I know that the lion can lie down with the lamb.
I guess blood's thicker than water, and even thicker than jam.

SUPER NAN

There's a lady I know, she's 90 or so,
And I sure think the world over her.
She's as strong as an ox and as cute as a fox,
And I know she's not lucky, no sir!

She won 649 five or six times,
And she won Super 7, yes, Bob.
But that's just for fun, and some cash on the side,
'Cause bingo's her regular job.

She can play 20 cards at the SUF Hall,
While she plays 45s on the side,
Open some tickets and enter a draw
For a two-gallon bottle of Tide.

Me, now, I've never won a thing in my life,
Never a bite of free lunch.
Well I s'pose that's a bit of a lie for me now—
I did win an ironing board once.

But the difference, you see, between Nanny and me,
Is her respect for this thing we call 'luck.'
She'll walk round a ladder and toss the spilled salt—
"You're superstitious, Nanny," says I, "to a fault."

"And that's what I'm not!" she snaps back at me,
Watching TV bingo in a trance.
"I'm not superstitious, not even a bit,
But I certainly won't take a chance."

"Nanny," I say, "I'll take you to Vegas,
Turn you loose in a casino or six.
Follow you 'round with two salt-beef buckets,
To hold all your money and chips.

"I dare say we'd be barred, by the crowd that's in charge,
And they'd be after you for a loan.
Then we'd have to go out and buy two or three semis
To haul all your money back home."

Now one day last fall, me and the wife's family
Were out to my nan's for a visit.
When a rabbit hopped by in front of her window,
"Oh, Nanny," I said, "how cute is it?"

"We'll see, now," she says, "just how cute he is."
And she jumped up from where she was sot.
"I'll tail a snare, and tomorrow, I dare
Say, I'll have that one into me pot."

Well, I sat up all night thinking about that bunny.
I'm a soft-hearted fellow, you see.
Now, don't get me wrong, I like meat, that's a fact,
As long as it comes from a styrofoam pack.

Next morning she was out in her kitchen with bottles,
"Oh, Nanny!" says I, feeling faint.
I'd hoped that poor bunny was still hopping about.
"Ha!" said my nan. "And that's what he ain't!"

And then there's time she was up on her roof
With a bucket of tar and a stick.
"Got a bit of a leak," she said, "David, my boy,
So I'm smearing it on pretty thick."

"Nanny!" says I, "get down out of that.
You shouldn't be up there, by rights!"
And I scravelled up with her, all manly and brave,
Even though I'm not too good with heights.

The next thing I knew I came all over giddy,
And started to whimper and whine.
Kicked over the tar, as I staggered about,
"Oh, Nanny!" I cried, before I passed out.

Not long after that the paper came out
With a picture of me and my nan.
I was slung over her shoulder, and the headline declared:
90-year-old Nan Rescues Man!

So this evening, you see, my nanny and me,
Will head to the SUF Hall.
She'll play 20 cards, as per usual,
And for me, well, one will be all.

The other players will mutter and moan and say,
"Might as well head on home."
Then one'll say, "Look! Buddy's with her tonight,
So she can't pay attention like when she's alone!"

"Was that B7, Nan?" "No, B11, my land!
David, you only got one card to play!"
"But there's too many numbers coming at me too fast,
And what's a postage stamp anyway, and what was that last
Number he called, oh, I wish he'd slow down,
And is there any other colour dabber—I don't much like brown?"

And so it will go, for the evening you see,
'Til my nan gets the jackpot, regardless of me.
And the 50-50 draw, and the bottle of Tide,
With the other players there just along for the ride.

And proper thing, says I, yes more power to her.
She's a tower of strength, that's how we all view her.
She'll tackle any job—she's courageous and plucky;
She's full of grace and good humour, and I know she's not lucky.

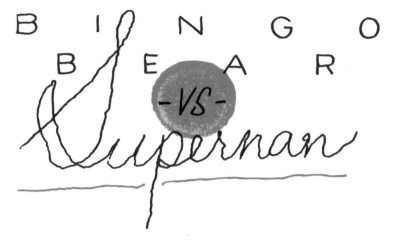

BINGO BEAR -vs- Supernan

Now 'twas bingo night in Boiler Cove, not so very long ago,
And Aunt Jose was some excited—she had one number left to go.
The caller waited for the ball, it seemed to take forever,
So she drank some Pepsi, braced herself, and thought, "'Tis now or never."

The jackpot was a thousand, and the hall was deathly still;
The also-rans were all mixed up, that would be Jim and Bill.
Aunt Josie had two dozen cards, and kept track of them all.
The boys had one between them, and even that was spoiled.

It seemed as if a lifetime passed before the ball was dropped.
Aunt Josie never blinked an eye; her breathing almost stopped.
And then the caller had the ball, and he held it up to see.
Then he looked out at the players and said, "Under the B."

"Under the B," he said again. "Under the B," once more.
And then he stuck his finger out, and pointed at the door.
Aunt Josie jumped up from her chair, and said, "My jumpins, Roy!
Never mind 'Under the B,' what number is it, b'y?"

But not a word came out of Roy, he sat there like a block.
"Roy," said Jim, "I'm all mixed up. You call B9 or not?"
And then Roy got his senses back and got his mouth in gear,
"A bbb.., a bbb...., a bbb..., a bear!"

The players finally turned around to saw what Roy had seen.
A polar bear was standing there, 'bout ten feet tall and mean.
He showed his teeth, he clicked his claws, he let the great big roar.
And just like that all hands jumped up and scravelled out the door.

Well, not quite all, my friends, you see, there were still three remaining.
Roy was frozen to his chair, and Josie was complaining.
The thought she'd lose the big jackpot tormented her, and drove her.
Then the bear walked up, looked at her cards, and said "Missus, move over!"

Now, Josie wasn't one to be afraid of much in life,
And Uncle Jim would often say, "Don't try and cross the wife."
But neither was she stunned, and so she up and crossed the hall.
The bear sat down, looked at the cards, and said, "Now caller, CALL!"

Roy finally had his vocals back, his eyes upon the door,
"B3," he squeaked, and then jumped up and took off up the Shore.
"Bingo!" said the grinning bear, "I guess the jackpot's mine."
He grabbed the cash, drank Josie's drink, and left poor Jose behind.

After that no bingo game was safe from Bingo Bear—
All up and down the Southern Shore, the people lived in fear.
He'd win the prizes, the 50-50 draw he always drew,
And if 'twas any cold plates on the go, he's always have them, too.

And it wasn't only bingo spoiled, if that was what you thought:
He'd go to card games at the home, get seniors all upsot.
He'd go 15 when he had a 5, it seemed like just for spite,
And he wouldn't trump with a whist to the board, and you know
                    now that's not right.

And then one night when Bill and Sooze had on the hockey game,
He came in through their picture window, broke out every pane.
He drank their beer, ate their grub; he left the place in ruins.
Bill used to be a Boston fan, but now he hates the Bruins.

The Wildlife wouldn't touch the bear, the Mounties stayed away.
The politicians wrung their hands, and said, "'tis bad, I'd say!"
With desperation at the breaking point for far too long,
The call went out across the land for a hero, brave and strong.

All hands was in a terrible state, until one night last fall,
They hadn't seen the bear awhile, so gathered at the hall.
Jose was doing good, with Jim and Bill, the usual torments;
They only had one card again, and that was all arseformance.

Then with one number left to go, the door flew open wide,
And Bingo Bear let out the roar, and then he stepped inside.
He challenged all to step outside, but found there were no takers;
He ate ten cold plates, 15 squares, and drained the coffee makers.

Then he walked around the tables, checking every card.
He stopped by Josie, said "Aha!" Josie said, "My lard."
The bear said, "On your feet right now. I wants those cards, my dear."
But then another voice rang out, "Now then, Mister Bear!"

All hands looked 'round to see who'd spoke in tone so strong and stern,
And when they saw her standing there, they felt their hope return.
She was the stuff of legends in bingo halls worldwide,
And she wore a pearl-handled dabber in a holster on her side.

The stories that were told of her were filled with awe and wonder—
Of how she'd played six dozen cards and never missed a number;
Of how she'd cleaned out Vegas one time, there on her own,
And how the crowd that ran the place came to her for a loan.

Supernan walked over and stood there face to face,
('Cause Bingo Bear, you know, he was still seated in his place).
"Now you," she said, "I heard about the trouble you been causin'.
You better stop that racket now. Be quiet and haul your claws in."

"Who's gonna make me?" roared the bear. "I'm king of all the halls.
I plays six dozen cards one time and don't miss either call."
The crowd was hushed, but those who heard him spoke 'll
Tell you, 'twas the first they ever heard him talking like a local.

"Mind now!" said Supernan, "You thinks you're pretty good.
How 'bout we have a jackpot game? That's if you think you could.
We'll both play with 100 cards, if you think you can manage.
Whoever loses leaves this place to be forever banished."

Well, Bingo Bear looked doubtful, and his brow began to sweat.
(Well I s'pose it did, 'twas hard to say, but the fur looked kind of wet.)
He knew that if if he backed down now, his name would be manure.
Besides, he liked the Southern Shore, and so he'd face on to her.

Then up he jumped, the table thumped, and said, "Alright, you're on!"
And then they stood there, face to gut: they were at dabbers drawn.
Two hundred cards were all laid out on top of two large tables.
The crowd was hushed—they knew 'twas one of bingo's greatest fables.

Aunt Jose said she'd go caller, if 'twas no disputin'.
The bear said, "Good enough, I s'pose, but I knows for who you're rootin'."
A retired history teacher from the home, whose name was Moore,
Loudly bawled, "Cry havoc and release the balls of war!"

And then the game commenced and the dabbers started flyin'.
Uncle Jim was on the tickets, but no one wasn't buyin'.
The players both were keeping up, as Josie called the numbers,
And Uncle Bill went back and got them Freshie in two tumblers.

By and by, with half the numbers called, the seniors drifted off
To have a game of 45s and get themselves a scoff.
A crowd had come from up the Shore to watch the bingo titans,
But in the fuss they missed one thing, the game was that excitin'.

Supernan and Bingo Bear were even up 'til then.
The dabbers flew. They dried a few; they used up nine or ten.
But then the bear began to swear though he never smelled a rat.
'Cause Supernan was after turning up the thermostat.

Then Bingo's eyes got full of sweat and he missed out on B2.
"Oh, what a sin," said Supernan, "I'll dab that one for you."
Then panic rose in Bingo's throat, he barely could hang on.
Out-played, out-psyched, and rendered out, the bear was almost gone.

Our hero played her trump card, then, an ace of hearts she laid.
And now I s'pose you're all mixed up 'cause bingo's what they played.
And you'd be right, for sure, but there's no way that you'd have known.
That she was also in the card game with the seniors from the home.

I'll say one thing for Bingo Bear—he knew when he was beaten.
But he never thought a 90-year-old missus would defeat him.
The cheers went up for Supernan, in the limelight she was basking:
The hero of the Southern Shore, the queen of multitasking.

She's back home now, and still goes out to bingo Tuesday nights.
But only plays a dozen cards, she don't like starting fights.
But she'll always come and help you out if your game is gone to rot,
'Cause some big ooonshik's acting bad and got all hands upsot.

As for Bingo Bear, you know, he left the Southern Shore.
He's playing chess in Finland now, but finds it all a bore.
He joined a barbershop quartet, but never sings in key,
And there's no bingo, squares, or cold plates up in Helsinki.

Well, the scratch in the back of my throat when I woke was certainly a pretty good clue,
So I woke up my wife, the love of my life, and said, "I think I'm getting the flu."

"Oh, yeah," she said, somewhere in the bed, not showing a lot of concern.
"But I'll be alright," I heroically said, "if I don't take too bad of a turn."

Now one thing upon which all husbands agree, as they go through their married lives,
Is that the colds and the flus, by which they're abused, are always much worse than their wives'.

Their wives' flus, I mean, which are never as mean as the colds and the flus that men get.
How else to explain that *they* seem just the same, whatever kind of bug that they get?

But new research shows something I suppose that men already know well,
That the male cold virus is ten times as vicious as the female, and so ten times the hell.

Take, for example, this miserable bug with which I am presently struck:
Symptoms include eyeballs which protrude, high fever, and a nose full of muck.

A casual survey indicates scurvy, measles, smallpox, and mumps.
My diagnosis means rum in small doses with Pepsi, delivered by pumps.

As I lie on the sofa, flirting with coma, I can feel yellow fever develop;
A hazmat team now arrives on the scene and erects a clear plastic envelope.

As I slip in and out of delirium, bouts of TB and malaria shake me.
If I wasn't so stoic and nobly heroic, any one of these conditions might take me.

As I battle with croup, I appeal for soup in the name of microbial defeat.
"In a minute," says my wife, the love of my life, "right after *Coronation Street.*"

It's touch and go for a while, what with East and West Nile, but eventually the crisis recedes.
Medicine's advanced and treatments enhanced for all my new pathogen breeds.

Recovery is long 'til I am once again strong but what else would my dear wife expect of me?
I politely decline her offer to perform a radical, complete daybed-ectomy.

Now like any tough man, I do what I can when I'm struck with a cold or the flu.
But listen, you wives, stop rolling your eyes—they're harder on us than on you.

With a week to go to Christmas Day, the townies were all freaking,
As word went out across the air: "This is the mayor speaking.
A winter storm watch is declared, stay home beside your heaters.
We could be hit with ten, or even 15, centimetres."

The schools are closed, all flights called off, downtown is shut down mostly,
But Ryan and Eddie got our backs—they're watching this one closely.
The regiment is all deployed with standby generators
For all the downtown Tim's, and Mary Brown's got extra taters.

Bingo night is cancelled in all parish halls, they say,
But you can get your bingo fix in a hall out 'round the bay.
The service clubs are all shut down, no need to wonder why.
No one wants to risk it 'cept the Optimists, eh b'y.

Now, far be it from me to question public sentiment,
But it seems like our good winter sense is mostly gone and went.
The bayman shrugs and yawns and says, "A bit of snow, I s'pose."
The townie writes his will and screeches, "This is it, I knows!"

All the TV stations got a meteorologist—
He smoothly shows the highs and lows, and mesmerizes us.
He uses fancy maps and that to tell us we will freeze,
Frightens us with weather bombs and polar vortices.

But even if we ever got a proper dump of snow,
Not the usual bit of slush, but say three feet or so,
We'd still be trying to get to work from CBS to town,
Cursing on the High Roads crowd and calling them right down.

Sliding on our baloney skins, snow tires in the shed,
'Cause we put off changing over, trying to save a bit of tread.
Forgot to buy a scraper and beat up the credit card
Scraping out a three-inch hole in two-inch windshield ice so hard.

But the b'ys are at O'Brien's, and Fred's is open, too.
The crowd at PAL are flying, sure they got the power crew.
But no one else is on the go, so far as I can see,
The Crow's Nest called Song Circle off, that's what poisons me.

'Cause I was headed down for that, until the news came through,
To try this new one on for size, and have a cold one, too.
But there's no Joy down at the Nest to pour my beer to quaff,
Though I dare say Arthur Barrett's got the steps all shovelled off.

I saw Hassan from Syria out walking in the storm,
In parka, mitts, and skidoo boots; he knows how to keep warm.
He sees me coming down Long's Hill in sneakers and jean jacket;
I'm turning blue, my feet are froze, I just can barely hack it.

He watches cars go sliding by with summer tires screaming.
Distracted drivers on their phones, all California dreaming.
He asks, "Do you need help?" as I bivver and turn blue.
"I'll call 911," he says. "You must be new here, too."

Now, I have heard it said that when a miller flaps her wings
Down in the jungles of Brazil, it causes many things.
Like barometric pressure drops and hurricanes and that,
I s'pose that miller used to blow the Bullet off the track.

But I wonder if that miller ever thinks of what she causes,
In the brain of TV weather guy as on his map he draws his
Highs and lows, and proudly shows us why we should be worried.
And if we don't get a blizzard then we'll be severely flurried.

He got his half an hour on the evening news, I s'pose,
And then the news is mostly weather, too, and later on you knows,
We get it all again before we go to hit the sack,
At 6 o'clock tomorrow morn, we know that he'll be back.

But I'm not the type to panic; no, I wouldn't go that far.
But my bottled water stash could fill the Muskrat reservoir.
And if that megaproject turns out to be a bummer,
The batteries in my basement, sure, will get me through to summer.

And if Number 3 goes down once more this year in Holyrood,
I'll do my best to cut down my usage, like you would.
And if it's Dark NL again, I know that I'll be fine,
But sometimes a man must be a man, and so I'll draw a line—

I got a set of long johns and I know that I won't freeze,
With the thermostat turned right down low to 25 degrees.
But I'll rant and roar on open line, and stand up for my rights,
If I can't get online or run 10,000 Christmas lights.

Now way back in the podauger days, when I was just a youngster,
The hockey was our winter sport, and I know we had some fun, sir.
No matter what the weather was, each weekend was the same:
We'd all show up at Joby's house to watch the hockey game.

About half the town was for the Leafs, the other for the Habs;
I don't remember real fights, but lots of verbal jabs.
A few of us liked other teams, but people didn't mind us—
They figured we were strange, I s'pose, but probably mostly harmless.

But the NHL, for sure, was not the only game around;
We had a wicked team ourselves, for such a little town.
The Jets is what we called them, and they made the bad guys quake.
They were known and feared by all the teams from 'Strivver to Mud Lake.

Well, truth be told, there only were two other teams, I guess;
The Flyers and the Flames were kind of frightened, more or less.
The Flames were from the Valley, and the Flyers from Goose Bay—
Two great big towns in Labrador an hour's drive away.

I lived in Northwest River, which was only small, you see,
Though at the time 400 people didn't seem that small to me.
And though the town was friendly and the people really nice,
The numbers just weren't there to put a team out on the ice.

So we had to get creative to get our numbers up to par,
And in isolated Labrador we couldn't look too far.
So we got some guys from Goose Bay and from the Valley, too,
And finally had enough to go from one line up to two.

But never three, it seems to me, the Jets all played a lot.
We might be perished in the stands but the boys were always hot.
The Airport Restaurant was the sponsor, and so the story goes,
The boys were paid ten bucks a goal, free pizza, too, I s'pose.

And so we had our three-team league and I recall the names,
Woodward's Flyers from Goose Bay and from the Valley Vicker's Flames.
But our boys quickly got the name for putting pucks in nets:
The Northwest River-Happy Valley-Goose Bay Airport Restaurant Jets.

We had Michelin on the left wing, and Michelin on the right;
At centre we had Michelin, good speed but not much height.
On right defence was Michelin, with Michelin to his left;
Our goalie was a Michelin, too, p'raps Hayward, Dick, or Fred.

Now it wasn't only Michelins, but you'd believe me if I tried
To say we had a tire plant or p'raps a restaurant guide.
We also had McLeans, a Blake, and from the coast a Nitsman,
Don't know about the first two now, but Nitsman's close to Michelin.

And the coach was Maki Winters, well liked and well respected;
He'd let the boys know fast if play was not what he expected.
The manager was Cyril, who spent his summers salmon fishing,
A nicer man you'd never meet, but now we're back to Michelin.

On game night all hands would pile aboard Cecil Blake's old van;
No blizzard ever stopped a Northwest River hockey fan.
And though it might be minus 30 in midwinter, well, you know,
The arena in the Valley might be 35 below.

A noisy crowd is what we were, though always few in number.
And when our boys scored we'd stamp our feet, 'twas almost like the thunder.
Even when they didn't score, we'd stamp and yell and cheer,
Trying to keep from freezing—it was savage cold in there.

We'd all go 'cross to Mary Brown's when intermission came,
And try to get unthawed before we went back to the game.
'Cause there's nothing like the french fries and hot coffee when you're froze
And you got frostburn on your ears and on your nose and in your toes.

Then back into the arena with our chicken, chips, and drink,
With nose and ears and toes gone back from blue to pink.
The players back out on the ice, the face-off close at hand,
The excitement in the building almost more than you could stand.

'Twas the last game of the playoffs, see? The score was two to two.
The Jets had barely tied it up with goals from Chum and Goo.
The ref had barely dropped the puck, the Flames were quickly rushing;
The air was thick with tension—sure, the Stanley Cup was nothing.

The air was thick with something else for this, the final game,
And the longer that the game went on the thicker it became.
A mild spell was on the go: the temperature was soaring—
Visibility was down in fog and neither team was scoring.

With the ceiling at about five feet, there was scarce a man could see!
The taller players' heads poked out, looked liked stumps in snow to me.
The ref looked kind of doubtful, and we thought he'd shut her down;
He'd raise his whistle now and then, but didn't make it sound.

Then all at once the light went on behind the bad guys' net,
And though 'twas kind of hard to follow, there was no doubt a Jet
Had scored the winning goal just as the final whistle blew:
The game was done, the Jets had won, the score was three to two.

They'd also won the series, but the trophy sure looked odd
As the half-seen players raised it and it moved across the fog.
And as we piled aboard Cecil's van we sang a victory song,
Then piled back out again to push—his starter motor gone.

Who scored the winning goal? We found out later on that night.
Remember Michelin at the centre? Good speed, but not much height?
He'd had the height advantage as he skated 'neath the fog,
And scored an easy one, the goalie sprawled out like a log.

And so that was hockey night in Labrador back in my younger day.

The Jets were always on our minds, October through to May.

We thought a lot about our team, we were loyal as it gets

To the Northwest River-Happy Valley-Goose Bay Airport Restaurant Jets.

Give me an N!......

MAN OF LA MANCHE

Now I s'pose you all have heard about those alien abductions,
And you've drawn your own conclusions, or made your own deductions.
Or p'raps you yourself was taken once while driving in your car,
And you was probed and poked and woke up with this funny looking scar.

Well, what odds about it, sure, it happens all the time—
You might be down a kidney, but then, one will do you fine.
It happened to my buddy, and I s'pose perhaps I'll launch
Into the story of John Chidley on the bridge down in La Manche.

All hands was on the party at my other buddy Paul's;
There was beer and songs and stories, there was laughs and calls and bawls.
We were well into the wee hours, and no one was feeling pain,
When John left to go up the Shore with Bev and Eugene Kane.

It had been a wicked evening, on that they did agree;
As they passed along by Tors Cove, it was almost half past three.
Then John spoke up from in the back, and said he had to stop—
The pressure in his holding tank was almost to the top.

So Bev pulled off the road, and John said, "Won't be long now, Missus."
And Eugene fell asleep, while John attended to his business.
That business being complete, he went to open up his door,
And that's when things got awful queer up on the Southern Shore.

All at once our man was lit up by a green light in the sky.
"Good enough," was what he thought. "S'pose I'm on the starboard side."
But then a red light lit him up, away off in the north,
And so he closed the starboard door, and went to get in through the port.

But then a yellow light went on, and John was on two minds:
When it came to navigation lights, he only knew two kinds.
Bev had heard the door come to, and figured he was back;
She yawned and drove away and said, "Can't wait to hit the sack."

Our buddy John, meanwhile, had up and vanished from the scene—
He was nothing, only particles in Captain Kirk's transporter beam.
When he was all put back together, he told the skipper to his face,
He wasn't over fussy being all gone abroad in space.

Old Kirk said he was sorry, but that he had an excuse;
He wasn't after John, see, he was trying to get his moose.
They'd been searching with the scanner, and all at once his hopes had soared;
"Spock," he said, "down by that bridge. There's one to beam aboard."

But 'twas John, you see, just done his pee, and I s'pose, 'twas in the dark.
"You fooled me up," said he. "And sure, you're hunting in the park!"
"What!?" said Kirk. "I didn't know! Chekov, where's your eyes?
I know that Starfleet won't be cross if I lose the *Enterprise*."

And then they both went kind of quiet, both were hesitating;
"I know now," Mr. Spock sang out, "that's not some fascinating."
Old Kirk got all downhearted, and said he never meant to bring on
All the trouble he was in, and was the Wildlife man a Klingon?

Meanwhile, further up the Shore, the Kanes were finally home;
Gene woke up, and Bev sang out, "I never more will roam."
It was kind of quiet in the back, Gene said, "Now wake up, John."
He turned to look back for the man, and there the man was...gone!

"Now, where the devil did he go?" said Gene. "I'm sore perplexed."
"I wants me bed," said Bev. "With that man, I'm surely vexed."
They headed back along the road to see if they could see him;
Said Gene, "I s'pose he's still back on the bridge, but surely not still peeing?"

Back on board the *Enterprise*, John said, "Now Jim, relax.
You got no moose, and I won't tell, and that's the very facts.
You can beam me down, right in my bunk, of that I have no doubt,
But first I think you owe me one—I wants to try your ship out!"

"No sweat, my buddy," Kirk spoke up. "Sit down in my chair.
Just tell Sulu what you wants; sure he knows how she goes in gear.
How 'bout a flick around the sun, or p'raps to Mercury?
We could stop into my cabin there and get a cup of tea."

And so John aimed her out in space, and warp 3 he had set.
"How fast you got to go," he asked, "to get her planed off on the step?"
"Put her warp 9," he said, "that should be fast enough, or
P'raps, put both feet on the gas, Sulu—whatever she can suffer."

And so they went to roar around the universe a bit,
Got bogged down in a big black hole, but then got out of it.
John liked the *Enterprise* so well, "How much for one?" he said.
Then lights came on again for John, this time blue and red.

"Pull over, John," said Captain Kirk. "Oh my, I'm some afraid—
I got 12,000 dollars' worth of tickets still unpaid."
Next thing, Worf was on the bridge and he was looking mad;
He'd got laid off from Picard's ship and joined the Space Constab.

He said, "Have you been drinking on the bridge? Now don't be telling lies, sir.
In jig time I will hook you to the deep-space breathalyzer.
And where's your registration and your licence and insurance?
I could nail you for a bunch of stuff, sure I got all the warrants."

Then John spoke up, and said, "My son, I wants your autograph!"
He told some jokes, and gave old Worf the biggest kind of laugh.
"Kirk," Worf said, "I'll let you go, we'll meet again no doubt.
Here's one more ticket for your stash—you got a tail light out."

"Now, John," said Kirk, "you are the man! I owe you one, no fear."
"Go on," said John, "you let me drive your ship; I'd say we're square.
Just beam me right back down again, and I will say goodnight.
I dare say Bev and Gene are after getting quite the fright."

Next thing you know our man was in the back seat of Bev's car.
"How you getting on?" he said. Said Gene, "So there you are!
Where in the devil did you go? We were almost off the deep end."
"Don't mind that," said John. "What's you two at next weekend?

"I'm going on a trip with my new fishing buddy, Jim.
He got the wicked vessel, sure you'd get along with him.
So you can stay at home and watch those foolish old Blue Jays, or
Come out with me and Jim—we're going turring with a phaser."